A
COMPELLING
CASE

A COMPELLING CASE

Michael Underwood, 1916 -

St. Martin's Press
New York

Library of Congress Cataloging-in-Publication Data

Underwood, Michael.
    A compelling case / Michael Underwood.
          p.   cm.
      ISBN 0-312-02887-3
      I. Title.
    PR6055.V3C66   1989
    823′.914—dc19   89-4098
                                                        CIP

First published in Great Britain by Macmillan London
Limited.

First U.S. Edition

10 9 8 7 6 5 4 3 2 1

Prologue

'You do believe I'm innocent, don't you, Miss Epton?'

It was a question that always caused Rosa a mental squirm, for no answer short of 'I'll stake my life on it' was going to satisfy the client seeking such an assurance. She had long since discovered it was no use replying that it was the jury's view that mattered and not her own.

'But I still want *you* to believe I'm innocent,' was the invariable riposte to that evasion.

Robin Snaith, who was Rosa's senior partner, merely used to give her an indulgent smile whenever she brought up the subject.

'It's only natural,' he was inclined to say. 'Clients always want to feel that their solicitor is one hundred per cent committed to their cause. It's an emotional need. They're like a drowning man looking for something to cling to. And because you're an attractive girl they want to cling all the tighter.'

'So what's your answer?' Rosa had long ago asked him.

'I say that lawyers are not concerned with innocence, only with the quantum of proof in each case.'

'And that satisfies them?' she had enquired incredulously.

'Of course not, but I move on quickly while they're still pondering what I've said. Quantum is a particularly good word for distracting their minds . . .'

Over the years Rosa had come to accept that her femininity did indeed render her more vulnerable to this perilously loaded question. The fact was, however, that very few clients were innocent within the dictionary meaning of the word.

5

That didn't prevent her fighting hard to obtain their acquittal where the evidence against them fell short. To Rosa, as to most lawyers, innocence and being found not guilty were two different things. But try explaining that to an indignant client!

From the time she had joined Robin's firm as a clerk, he had always warned her against the dangers of becoming emotionally involved in a case. It was sound advice and she normally had no difficulty keeping her head firmly in control of her heart. Just occasionally, however, something would happen to disturb the balance and then the effect was apt to be felt all round the office, for she was not one to agonise in silence.

There was, moreover, the additional factor that whenever she did believe a client to be truly innocent, the task of defending him became that much more onerous.

The Queen against Stephen Lumley was such a case . . .

Chapter 1

'How'd things go in court today?'

Rosa glanced up to find Robin standing in her doorway. She had just returned from court and was still taking papers out of her briefcase.

She gave him a quizzical look. Her case had not been one in which he had any particular interest and that meant his enquiry was merely a pretext for finding out what sort of mood she was in. Which, in turn, meant he was about to ask her a favour if the moment seemed propitious. He always took trouble to choose the right moment for his approaches.

'They didn't,' Rosa said with a sigh. 'The chief prosecution witness failed to turn up and there was an adjournment. The police were livid as they'd visited him yesterday evening and he'd promised he'd be at court today.'

'A familiar story,' Robin observed. 'I take it your client's influence stretches beyond his garden wall?'

'He's King Kong without the charm. Need I say more! Anyway, what really brings you to my room?'

'May I offload a case on you?'

'Of course. Is that all? I thought you were about to tell me you'd been dipping into the clients' account. What case is it?'

'Lumley.'

'Is he the chap charged with armed robbery?'

'And with attempted murder. He came up on remand this morning and has been put over to next Thursday, which clashes with that case of mine involving the MP's wife, which is part-heard. So I must give it priority.'

'That's all right,' Rosa said cheerfully, glancing at her diary. 'I can manage Lumley that day. Tell me something about it.'

'Three men, of whom one is alleged to be our client, raid a jeweller's shop off Oxford Street. A shot is fired at the owner as he emerges from his office at the rear. The men grab about £100,000 worth of stuff, mostly diamond and sapphire rings, and flee. Two of the raiders got clean away, but Lumley was tripped up by a passer-by as he made his escape and was arrested.'

'Was he carrying a gun?'

'No.'

'That's something.'

'It's about all.'

'What about the two who got away, do the police have descriptions?'

Robin shook his head. 'It seems likely they were disguised. Wigs and false moustaches and that sort of thing.'

'And Lumley?'

'Not disguised.'

'Why should two have been disguised and not the third?'

'Lumley insists he wasn't part of the gang. He says he was an innocent who got caught up.'

'Why'd he run away then?'

'A good question. You'll be able to ask him. I've not had more than a five-minute chat with him.'

'What was he doing in the shop? Was he a bona fide customer?'

'He's a nephew of the owner, Bernard Hammond, and had gone there to see his uncle.'

'An unfortunate piece of timing!'

'Disastrous, if he's to be believed.'

'And do you believe him?'

Robin gave her a sardonic smile.

'Depending on the judge, I'd say he'll get between five and ten years.'

* * *

It wasn't long after Robin had returned to his own room that Stephanie, their telephonist-cum-receptionist, came on the line.

'I have a Mrs Lumley who'd like to speak to you,' she announced in her usual dispassionate voice. 'She asked for Mr Snaith, but I understand you're now handling the case involving her husband. Shall I put her through or tell her you're engaged?'

'No, I'll speak to her, Steph,' Rosa said. Having taken the case over she might as well plunge right in. She was going to need to talk to Mrs Lumley at some stage, though she would normally have waited until after she had met Stephen Lumley himself. She picked up her pen and pulled a thick note-pad toward her.

'Miss Epton?' a nervous voice enquired. 'I'm Christine Lumley. I gather you've taken over my husband's case.'

'That's right. My partner, Mr Snaith, is unable to attend court when your husband appears next week and has asked me to act in his place.'

'I'm ever so grateful to you.'

Rosa blinked in surprise. Defendants and their wives weren't noted for offering thanks to their lawyer – and certainly not at such an early stage of proceedings. In Rosa's experience, most of her clients regarded legal aid as their right; something supplied by the state and therefore not subject to any norms of gratitude.

'What can I do to help you, Mrs Lumley?' she asked.

'Stephen's innocent, Miss Epton. He really is. I hope you believe that.'

'Whatever I believe won't affect my efforts at defending him,' Rosa said in what she hoped was a reassuring tone. 'But at the moment I know very little about the case. In any event, courts are not concerned with innocence as such. They are there to weigh up all the evidence and then decide whether or not a charge is proved. If it's not, the defendant is found not guilty and goes free.'

'But surely it must make it easier for you to know your client is innocent?'

Rosa groaned inwardly. Christine Lumley sounded nice enough, but she would try Rosa's patience if she insisted on plugging her husband's innocence every time they spoke.

'I think the best thing would be for us to meet, Mrs Lumley,' she said briskly. 'Could you come to my office tomorrow afternoon at, say, three o'clock. Then we can discuss the case.'

Rosa wasn't due in court the next day and spent the morning working on papers in her office. It was two o'clock before she decided to go out for a quick lunch. There was a family-run Italian café nearby which she usually visited on such occasions. In summer a sandwich sufficed and in winter a steaming bowl of minestrone. Occasionally, very occasionally in view of its calorific content, she would have a plate of spaghetti bolognese.

On this particular November day she decided to break with routine and have a cheese omelette. She was a popular customer and was always greeted like a long lost relative by Mamma Capella and her dashing son, Paolo.

Finishing her cup of black coffee, she left money for the bill on the table and slipped away while mother and son were busy with other customers.

It was just after two thirty when she got back to the office. As she opened the outer door she became aware of a young woman sitting nervously on the edge of a chair in the small reception area. Stephanie's face, wearing an expression of sardonic despair, was framed in the hatch behind.

'Mrs Lumley?' Rosa enquired.

The girl jumped up. 'I'm afraid I'm early. I hope you don't mind.'

'That's all right. Come along to my room.'

'I've had to arrange for a neighbour to look after the children and I promised I'd be back by four thirty.'

'How old are they?'

'Maxwell's six and Cheryl's three. Max goes to school and Cheryl's just started at a play group three mornings a week.'

'Whereabouts do you live?'

'We've got a flat in Kilburn. It's not ideal, but . . . ' She gave a helpless shrug. 'Well, there's no point in thinking about moving at the moment, though Stephen and I had discussed getting away from London before all this happened. It's not a good environment for children. I come from Cambridgeshire myself.'

They had reached Rosa's room and were seated, Rosa behind her desk and Christine Lumley in a chair to one side. Rosa had always avoided having her visitors sitting directly opposite her as she felt it gave an unfortunate effect of confrontation.

'Let's get one or two questions out of the way first,' she said as she prepared to make notes. 'How old is your husband?'

'Twenty-nine. I'm twenty-six.'

'And what's his job?'

Christine Lumley bit her lip and looked suddenly close to tears. She was a nice-looking girl in an unspectacular sort of way. Her fair hair was cut short and she had neat features, though her eyes reflected the strain she was living under. They had a lack-lustre appearance and were surrounded by smudges of exhaustion.

'He's been out of work for some time,' she said. 'But I hope you won't hold that against him.'

'What used he to do when he was in work?'

'He's had a lot of different jobs. It hasn't always been his fault, but if Stephen takes a dislike to someone, he's apt to show it.'

'To an employer, you mean?'

She gave a nod. 'He's best working for himself. He enjoyed being a mini-cab driver, but then he had an accident and the insurance company refused to pay up and he couldn't afford to put the car back on the road. That was an absolute disaster. Since then, he's just done anything that came to hand, which means we've not had a regular income.' Rosa waited for her to go on, which she did with obvious painful recollection of the difficult times they'd been through. 'Like everyone else we have our money problems. We're in debt all round. And now this nightmare!' She paused; then giving Rosa an almost defiant look she said, 'But Stephen's innocent. You must believe that. Being charged and held in prison has shattered him. I've never known him so depressed.'

'Has he ever been in trouble before?'

'Not since we got married seven years ago,' she said, with a returning note of defiance.

'But before that?'

'He was in court a couple of times. Once for burglary when he was only eighteen and then a year or so later he was involved in a stupid fight with other youths outside a club. He was charged with assault and with carrying an offensive weapon. But he wasn't sent to prison either time and he's gone straight ever since I've known him.' She blinked away a tear. 'He may have been a bit wild as a youth, but that's all in the past and he's been a good husband and father.'

Rosa stared thoughtfully at her note-pad for a while. Then looking up, she said, 'How did he come to get involved in the armed robbery at Hammond's?'

'He wasn't part of it,' she said vehemently. 'It was a ghastly coincidence that he was there when it took place.' She shot Rosa a challenging look. 'Coincidences do happen, Miss Epton.'

Rosa was also well aware how awkward they were to explain away in a court where a defendant's evidence in particular tended to be regarded with a degree of scepticism.

Christine Lumley now went on, 'Bernard Hammond is Stephen's uncle. Stephen went to see him that morning to ask him to lend us some money.' Her voice had become taut with emotion. 'He had lent us money in the past, but . . . ' She paused as though suddenly unable to articulate her words. 'The last time Stephen went to see him, they had a row and Uncle Bernard told him not to come bothering him again.'

'How long ago was that?'

'Around the end of July. Just before last Christmas Uncle Bernard got married for the third time and Carol, his new

12

wife, turned him against us. She's at least twenty years younger than he is and had worked in the shop for several years. She lost no time in getting him to marry her once his second wife had died.'

Her tone told Rosa all she needed to know about the third Mrs Hammond.

'Which side of the family does Uncle Bernard come from?'

'He's Stephen's mother's brother. Stephen's parents were killed in a car crash soon after we were married and Uncle Bernard is his only relative.'

Rosa stared pensively at her notes for a moment. 'Am I right in thinking that, as far as the robbery is concerned, all you know is what Stephen himself has told you?'

'Yes, but I know he's told me the truth. He wanted to patch up his quarrel with Uncle Bernard. That was why he went to see him.'

Rosa decided not to challenge what struck her as a somewhat disingenuous remark.

'When did you first learn about the robbery?' she asked.

Christine Lumley gave a shudder. 'When the flat was suddenly full of policemen. They turned the place upside down despite my protests. One of them told me Stephen had been caught red-handed on an armed raid and was under arrest. There was a woman officer with them and she tried to be kind when she saw how upset I was.'

Rosa nodded sympathetically. 'I think that's as far as we can go at the moment, Mrs Lumley. I'll see Stephen at court next week and have an opportunity of hearing what he has to tell me— '

'Couldn't you go and see him before?' she broke in. 'He's in Wormwood Scrubs. I know a visit from his solicitor would help his morale. He spends practically the whole day locked in his cell and it's driving him mad. He counts the minutes until his release. That shows he's innocent. If he'd done what the police say, he wouldn't fret the way he does.'

Rosa sighed. 'All right, I'll try and go to see him in the next few days. Mind you, there's very little I can do until the prosecution serve us with the statements of the witnesses on whom they're relying to prove the charges. Until then, it's simply a matter of waiting.' She gazed steadily at the woman sitting nervously forward in her visitor's chair. 'I'm afraid you must be prepared for a long wait before the case reaches a conclusion, so you must be steadfast for your husband's sake and patient for mine.'

Christine Lumley gave Rosa a bleak look. 'But that's terrible when I know he's innocent.'

Rosa thought it kinder to refrain from comment.

Chapter 2

The following Monday afternoon Rosa paid her promised visit to Wormwood Scrubs. Of all London's prisons the Scrubs was the nearest to her office, though that was about the only thing in its favour.

Used as she was to visiting clients in prison, she still found it a grimly depressing experience. However liberal their régimes compared with half a century ago, it was still like entering a different world. She felt that only the totally unimaginative could survive unscarred. For most it was an existence to be endured as best one could. Those who complained that prison life was soft (too soft) had no conception of the effect a lengthy deprivation of liberty could have. For the normal person, even though society had branded him a criminal, imprisonment was a traumatic experience.

Such were her thoughts as she sat in one of the interview cubicles in the 'legal visits hall' waiting for Stephen Lumley to appear. For a brief moment the sound of doors being unlocked and re-locked was over and she sat in silence.

The door of the cubicle opened and a young man came in. His escorting officer closed the door behind him, but didn't enter.

Being a remand prisoner, Stephen Lumley was wearing his own clothes and was dressed in a black windcheater with a pale blue T-shirt beneath and a pair of jeans. Presumably, Rosa reflected, what he'd been wearing when he went to Uncle Bernard's shop that fateful morning two weeks before.

'Christine told me you'd be along, so I knew it must be you when they said I had a legal visitor.'

He sat down and faced Rosa across a small table rather as if they were about to embark on a game of chess. He had fair, slightly reddish hair cut short to reveal a well-shaped head. His eyes were a nondescript grey and he had a bud-like lower lip. It was a day or so since he had shaved and the stubble on his chin and upper lip reflected the red in his hair.

'Your wife has told me all she can about what happened,' Rosa said, 'but only you, of course, can provide the detail.'

'I'm innocent, Miss Epton. The police have blundered.'

'If you're innocent, why did you run away? It's a question that's going to be thrown at you over and over again. It's not the sort of conduct a court is likely to associate with innocence.'

He stared vacantly into a corner of the room before replying.

'I was scared. I panicked,' he said, not meeting her gaze. 'I lost my nerve when Uncle Bernard suddenly came out of the room at the back and saw me there. It was his expression that did it.'

'Describe it.'

'He obviously thought I was one of the gang. There was a look of shock and outrage on his face.'

'At what point was the shot fired?'

'Then, as he was staring at me.'

'Whereabouts were the other two in relation to yourself?'

'We were more or less standing in a row.'

'Did you see which of them fired the gun?'

'I think it was the one next to me. The whole thing was over in a minute. The one further from me was shovelling stuff from the showcase into a bag.'

'How did he open the showcase?'

'He smashed the glass with a heavy hammer.'

'About how long had you been in the shop before all this happened?'

'No time at all. I'd just asked Susan, who was the assistant behind the counter, whether my uncle was there when they

16

came bursting in. One pointed the gun at Susan while the other smashed the showcase.'

'Did they take any notice of *you*?'

Lumley fidgeted uncomfortably. 'They were too intent on their business.'

'And as they made good their escape, you ran off too?'

'Yes. I was scared out of my wits and wasn't thinking straight.'

'How were they dressed?'

'They both had large moustaches. One was wearing a black hat with a brim, the other a green tweedy hat turned down all round.'

'Your wife said they were wearing wigs.'

'They each had shoulder-length hair and I reckon they must have been wigs. I remember thinking it didn't look normal.'

'Have you any idea who they were?'

'I've never seen either of them before in my life. I swear that's the truth.'

'Apart from your wife, did anyone know you were intending to visit the shop that morning?'

'I phoned to find out that Uncle Bernard would be in that day.'

'Who did you speak to?'

'Philip. He and Susan are the two counter assistants. He confirmed that my uncle was at the shop.'

'Did you ask him to give your uncle a message?'

Lumley shook his head, apparently embarrassed by the question.

'No. I didn't tell him who was speaking and I doubt whether he'd have recognised my voice.'

'But if you recognised his, it's a reasonable assumption that he recognised yours.'

'I just assumed it was Philip. I knew it wasn't Uncle Bernard's voice.'

'And when you fled, were you behind or in front of the other two?'

'Behind. They got into a waiting car and drove off at high

speed. I ran along the pavement until somebody tripped me and I fell. The next thing I knew, I had three men sitting on top of me and then the police arrived.' He paused. 'I swear that's the truth, Miss Epton.'

But is it the whole truth, Rosa wondered. She was used to clients who wove a cunning tapestry of truth, half-truths and downright lies. The coincidence of his arrival at the shop just before the raid was difficult to accept. And even if accepted, what about his flight? He was certainly going to need a sympathetic, not to mention gullible, jury.

'Did you make a written statement to the police?' she asked, closing her notebook.

'Yes. I hoped it would stop them charging me.'

'Is there anything in it you haven't told me?'

'No, definitely not.'

'Well, I'll see you at court on Thursday.'

'Any chance of bail?'

'I'd say, absolutely none.'

'I thought everyone was innocent until proved guilty,' he said bitterly.

'They are, but I'm afraid you still won't get bail.'

She opened her handbag and took out a packet of cigarettes and two bars of milk chocolate, which she pushed across the table towards him.

'Thanks,' he said with a distracted air. Then, with a smile dredged up from his boots, he added, 'And thanks for coming this afternoon.'

Robin was talking to Stephanie when Rosa got back to the office.

'Well,' he enquired, 'how do you rate his chances?'

'Maybe a bit higher than you do, but not much. However, these are early days.'

Something in her tone warned Robin that her terrier instinct had been aroused and he exchanged a wry look with Stephanie.

Chapter 3

'No point in my coming to court tomorrow,' Detective Superintendent Forrester said. 'It's only a formal remand. Bit of a waste of your time too, Ian, but you'd better be there to hold the hand of whoever turns up from the CPS.'

His tone held a note of scorn. Ever since the creation of the Crown Prosecution Service, things had been chaotic, largely due to under-manning and the right hand all too often not knowing what the left was up to. Teething problems, said the optimists. May have looked all right on paper, said the sceptics, but it'll never be made to work.

Detective Inspector Ian Cleave, who was Forrester's second-in-command on the Lumley case, made to leave, but his Detective Superintendent went on, 'Have a quiet word with Lumley's solicitor. Mention that Lumley would be doing himself a favour if he gave us the names of his co-conspirators. Nobody's going to believe that he doesn't know their identities and one way or another we've got to extract the information out of him. Anyway, plant the seed in his solicitor's ear. Snaith, isn't it?'

'When I was at the Scrubs yesterday, I heard from one of the screws that he'd been visited by Snaith's partner, Rosa Epton.'

Forrester pulled a face. 'That's bad news. She can be an obstructive little cow when she puts her mind to it.'

DI Cleave nodded solemnly. Personally he rather liked Rosa and respected her fighting qualities. Not that he could envisage much scope for a fight in the present case. Lumley had been caught red-handed and there was enough evidence to put him away for a long spell.

'Anyway,' Forrester continued, 'even if Miss Epton is defending, no reason not to sound her out. She's bright enough to see where her client's best interests lie.' He lit a cigarette and inhaled luxuriously. 'At least we got a statement out of Lumley before busy little Miss Epton arrived on the scene.'

'I was just coming to look for you,' Rosa said to DI Cleave when she bumped into him at court the next morning.

'Snap!' he remarked with a smile.

Not for the first time it struck her that he resembled a friendly young bank manager of the sort more usually met in TV advertisements than in real life.

'I hadn't realised you were involved in Lumley until the jailer told me just now. My client only mentioned Superintendent Forrester.'

'He's the big white chief. I'm the proverbial side-kick.'

They were standing in a narrow passage in which defendants were being marshalled for their appearance in court. First on were the drunks and prostitutes who would be in and out as rapidly as if they were on a conveyor belt. It was not the best place for quiet conversation.

'Let's get out of here and find somewhere we can talk,' Rosa said, as one of the drunks lurched against her, treading heavily on her foot and treating her to a blast of his dragon's breath.

'Why don't we go to the café round the corner? I'll let the jailer know where we are. The overnight charges will take at least forty-five minutes, so we shan't be called on for some time.'

Five minutes later they were seated at a corner table with two cups of coffee which Cleave had insisted on buying.

'What can you tell me about the case that my client is unlikely to have told me?' Rosa said with a wry smile.

'With all respect to you, Miss Epton, I'd say Lumley's about as guilty as they come. I know he says he's the innocent victim of cruel circumstances, but the facts speak for themselves. If I may say so, there's only one way he can help himself and that's to tell us the names of the other two men.'

'He assures me he has no idea who they were.'

Cleave sighed. 'I know that's been his line to date, but it's not going to get him very far. However, if he wants to take all the blame . . . ' He paused, before adding, 'You know he has form?'

'That was a long time ago. He's gone straight since he's been married.'

'When the pressure's on, people are apt to revert to type.'

'Meaning?'

'We know he's in financial straits. Debts all round and creditors becoming more threatening by the week. The raid on Hammond's netted over £100,000. Split that three ways and it's still a tidy sum for each of them.'

'Is there any evidence that Lumley has benefited financially?'

'No, but that doesn't mean his share's not being looked after for him.'

It was apparent that Cleave had no doubts at all about Stephen Lumley's participation in the crime. She hadn't seriously expected otherwise.

'I gather the two unidentified men were wearing disguises,' she now said.

'That's what we believe from what we've been told.' He smiled. 'I know what you're going to say next, Miss Epton. Why wasn't your client also disguised?'

'Well, why wasn't he?' Rosa said, faintly nettled at having her question pre-empted.

'It could have been a clever move on his part.'

'It doesn't sound very clever to me.'

'The odds are that he'd probably have been recognised even if he'd put on a wig and a bushy black beard. After all, he was known to everyone in the shop. My own theory is that he played a sort of decoy role. And, anyway, innocent people don't run away.' He paused and gave his coffee a thoughtful stir. 'At the moment, Lumley's charged with armed robbery and with attempted murder, but we're going to suggest to counsel that he should also face a charge of conspiring with persons unknown to commit these crimes.'

21

'That seems a bit heavy-handed.'

Cleave gave a shrug. 'Of course if he told us the names of his co-conspirators, it might alter things. Look, Miss Epton, if he's keeping silent out of fear, he has no need to. I'm sure you'll be telling him that it's every man for himself in this sort of situation.' He glanced at his watch. 'Perhaps we ought to be getting back to court.'

If the police *were* right and Lumley *did* know the identities of the other two men, Rosa could still think of reasons why he should deny this, the main one being that he would almost certainly forfeit his share of the spoil if he grassed. On the other hand, he hadn't given her the impression of someone comfortable in the knowledge that his wife would be provided for while he was in prison.

'How soon do you expect to let me have the statements?' she asked as they walked back to court.

Pulling a face, he said, 'If there's any delay it won't be our fault. You know how things are with the CPS in London, pretty chaotic. I take it you'll accept a paper committal.'

'I can't say until I've read the statements.'

'Surely it's not the sort of case you'd fight in the lower court?'

'The sooner I get the statements, the sooner I'll let you know,' she replied crisply, causing Cleave to reflect that perhaps Superintendent Forrester was right in his assessment of her.

Their return was well timed and Rosa had scarcely taken her seat in court when the case was called on. Stephen Lumley stepped into the small railed dock and stared stonily ahead of him.

'Yes, which case is this?' the magistrate enquired grumpily, looking up from the seed catalogue he'd been surreptitiously studying. He'd been on the bench a great many years and wasn't renowned for his even temper.

'Lumley, your worship,' the jailer announced with a shade of impatience, there being little love lost between magistrate and court staff.

'Yes . . . well, I haven't got all morning,' the magistrate

said, casting a bilious look around his court. 'Who's appearing?'

'I represent the defendant, your worship,' Rosa said, jumping to her feet when it became apparent that nobody else was going to step into the breach.

'Is there nobody here from the prosecution service? What am I being asked to do in this case?' His gaze roamed the court like that of a superannuated rhinoceros looking for easy prey.

DI Cleave hurried into the witness-box. 'I'm the officer in the case, your worship,' he said quickly. 'I was expecting there'd be somebody here from the Crown Prosecution Service, but they don't seem to have turned up.'

'Well, I can't wait all day. What do you want, a further remand?'

'If you please, your worship.'

'Yes, very well.' Glancing in Rosa's direction, he went on, 'You're not applying for bail, are you? Anyway I'm not prepared to consider bail in a case involving such serious charges. There'll be a further remand in custody.' Then, muttering something to his clerk, he rose to his feet and ambled off the bench.

'The court is adjourned for ten minutes,' the clerk announced in a resigned tone.

'He pretends he has digestive problems,' Cleave murmured to Rosa. 'But everyone knows he's gone off to his room for a cigarette. He can't get through the morning without a break. At least he doesn't smoke cigars.'

Rosa had promised to have a further word with Lumley after the hearing and she now returned to the jailer's office. He was in a cell standing with his back to the door. When he turned round, he was wearing a stern but vulnerable look, rather, she imagined, like the boy who had stood on the burning deck.

'How can that old bastard behave like that and get away with it?' he said bitterly.

'I'm afraid some magistrates get that way. They are lords of all they survey and that can become very corrupting over the years.' She paused. 'I didn't see your wife in court. Was she there?'

He shook his head. 'She comes to the prison most days. As a remand prisoner, I'm allowed one fifteen-minute social visit every day. But I've told her never to bring the kids. I don't want them to know where their dad is.'

Rosa silently hoped they need never find out, though should he be convicted and sentenced to a long term of imprisonment, it was going to place an intolerable strain on his family ties. She'd seen it so often before and it never failed to distress her. The fact was that prison was destructive of almost everything that mattered in a human relationship and no amount of 'do-gooding' could alter the situation.

'I'll be in touch with you just as soon as the prosecution serve us with the statements of their witnesses,' she said, breaking the silence that had fallen between them. 'Meanwhile, I shan't be entirely idle.' He shot her a questioning look and she went on, 'There are several enquiries I can be making. At Bernard Hammond's, for a start.'

Chapter 4

Rosa decided that Saturday afternoon would provide a good opportunity for reconnoitring Uncle Bernard's shop in Firley Street. She could combine the visit with her normal weekend shopping expedition. A carrier bag of groceries in her hand would deflect suspicion from the real purpose of her being there, for she didn't propose to declare her identity. A broken necklace she seldom wore would give her an excuse to enter the shop. Let Bernard Hammond and Co have the pleasure of her custom!

She found Oxford Street thronged with its usual Saturday afternoon shoppers and was glad to escape from its crowded pavements. Grizzling children in push-chairs and people more laden than pack-mules were a test of anyone's patience. Firley Street ran parallel to the main thoroughfare on its north side a few hundred yards along from Marble Arch.

Walking past a sandwich bar, a betting shop and something called 'Cleopatra's Bathroom Emporium' she came upon 'Bernard Hammond and Co, High-Class Jewellers and Goldsmiths'.

It was a double-fronted shop and she paused to look in its windows. It obviously wasn't as up-market as the jewellers to be found in the area of Bond Street, but, equally, more exclusive than those that abounded in suburban high streets.

Uncle Bernard's windows weren't full of glitzy baubles; on the other hand she doubted whether he stocked diamond tiaras.

She tried the door, but found it locked. Then a typed

notice on the glass panel caught her eye. 'Please ring bell to enter.' She did so and almost immediately the door buzzed open.

There was a counter straight ahead with a young female assistant standing behind it watching her.

'I'm afraid I didn't see the notice at first,' Rosa said, with a smile.

'It's part of our new security,' the girl replied. 'You may have read about it, we had an armed robbery here about two weeks ago.'

'Were you here when it happened?'

The girl gave a small shiver and nodded.

'It was all over so quickly that one didn't have time to be scared until afterwards.' She glanced anxiously at a curtained-off doorway behind, then lowering her voice, went on, 'What made it worse was recognising one of the robbers ... '

Before she could say anything further, the curtain was pulled aside and a blonde head appeared. The woman gave Rosa a suspicious look, before turning to the girl and saying, 'I'll serve this customer, Susan. You have your tea-break.'

The girl nodded and scuttled out of sight.

'May I help you?' the woman enquired of Rosa, who felt certain that she must be the third Mrs Hammond.

'I have a necklace that needs repairing,' Rosa said, producing it from her handbag. 'The clasp has broken.'

Carol Hammond gave it a quick look. 'We don't normally undertake repairs of this sort. I suggest you try one of the trade jewellers in Oxford Street.' Perhaps because she thought she had been unnecessarily brusque she added, 'The man we used to employ for repairs has retired and craftsmen of that sort are irreplaceable, so we'd have to send it away in any event.' She completed her explanation and gave Rosa a small wintry smile.

'I'll try somewhere else,' Rosa said, returning the smile in kind and picking up her shopping bag.

She walked along the pavement and turned into the sandwich bar which was open but empty. It had a number of bar stools to accommodate a few customers at one end of the counter. There was a youth clearing up behind and she ordered a cup of tea and a Danish pastry.

'What time do you close?' she asked.

'Half four on a Saturday,' he said, without glancing up.

'Were you here when Hammond's was robbed the other day?'

This time he did look up from what he was doing. 'Yes. But it was all over before we knew what had happened.'

'You didn't hear the shot that was fired?'

He shook his head. 'No, though Mario – he's the boss – pretended he had when he thought he was going to appear on TV.' He laughed. 'Are you a reporter?' he added hopefully.

'Afraid not. It's just that I went into Hammond's a few minutes ago and there seemed to be a bit of atmosphere.'

'You can say that again. Susan – she's an assistant in the shop – comes in here most days and she says it's as if they're all under suspicion. Old Hammond himself is all right, but it's his wife. She's told them not to talk to anyone about what happened. Says it's because they're witnesses, but Susan feels there's more to it than that. There's a rumour that an ex-associate of old Hammond's could have been behind the robbery. Can't remember his name, but Mr Hammond is supposed to have driven him into bankruptcy and he's borne him a grudge ever since. Anyway that's Mrs Hammond's theory.'

'I think it must have been she who served me,' Rosa remarked.

'Blonde woman with eyes that could cut through steel?'

'You could say that,' Rosa said with a laugh. 'Are the police following up this angle?'

'I reckon they must be following up every angle on offer. After all, they only ever caught one chap. He fell over as he was escaping and a heavyweight from the block of flats along the road sat on him until the police arrived. The other two men got clean away.' He glanced at his watch. 'If you've finished, I'll lock up and go home. Taking my girlfriend out tonight.'

Rosa finished her tea and pushed her half-eaten Danish pastry to one side. 'Do you happen to know what time Hammond's close on Saturdays?'

'Five. Why? Going back there, are you?'

'Yes, I've remembered I need a new watch strap.'

The youth gave her a cheeky grin. 'You are a reporter, aren't you?'

'Sort of,' Rosa replied with a conspiratorial smile as she slid off her stool and moved towards the door.

Crossing the road she walked along the pavement on the other side. There was a number of small shops whose windows she was able to study without attracting attention. One of them, a smart boutique, had a dress on display that took her fancy. It was burgundy red and made of wool, cut simply with an embroidered motif at the left shoulder. It was just what she needed for winter parties. But the boutique was closed and wasn't the sort of establishment to hang vulgar price tags on its clothes. She turned away with a sigh and glanced across at Hammond's on the opposite side just as an elderly, smartly dressed man came out and strode away along the pavement. He had an ardent, dashing air about him as if he was off to meet a floosie with a well-chosen present in his pocket.

She walked on a further thirty yards, glancing continually over her shoulder to make sure she didn't miss Susan's departure from work. Returning to Hammond's side of the street, she walked slowly towards the shop. She reckoned the girl would leave a few minutes either side of five o'clock, and it was now four minutes before.

Pausing two doors away, she gave half-hearted attention to a window full of Persian rugs. Then she noticed an assistant moving towards the door, presumably to coax her inside and she hurried away. He gave her a melancholy look as she fled. Perhaps she was the nearest he'd come to a sale that day.

Suddenly Hammond's door opened and Susan came out. Without glancing in Rosa's direction she walked off the other way. Rosa quickened her own pace and drew level with her outside the sandwich bar.

'Excuse me,' she said a trifle breathlessly. 'I was hoping to catch you. Can we talk somewhere? It really is important and I promise not to hold you up very long.'

The girl stared at her with a puzzled frown. 'You were in the shop this afternoon,' she said with a dawning look. 'I knew your face, but for a second couldn't place you.'

'Mrs Hammond sent you off for your tea-break. I got the impression she didn't approve of our talking.'

'She's suspicious of everyone and everything since the robbery.'

'It's concerning the robbery that I'd like to speak to you. Can you spare a few minutes? I'd be most grateful.'

'All right, but let's get away from here. I don't want Mrs Hammond to see me when she leaves.'

Five minutes later they reached Marble Arch and entered the portals of the Cumberland Hotel, where they were quickly submerged in a sea of anonymous faces.

'I thought there was something funny about you,' Susan Cunliffe said after they had found somewhere to sit down. 'I don't mean that rudely, but I felt you had an ulterior motive.'

'Did Mrs Hammond also suspect something, do you think?'

'She never said anything after you'd gone, but from the way she interrupted us, she may have done.' She gave Rosa an appraising look. 'So you're a solicitor! It must be much more interesting than working in a shop.'

'I imagine we both have our frustrations,' Rosa said and went on, 'I gather you knew Stephen Lumley by sight?'

'I'd seen him once or twice when he came to the shop.' She bit her lip. 'Is it all right my talking to you about the case. I mean, I've given a statement to the police and been told I'll be a witness.'

'I'm not saying the police wouldn't try and prevent you from talking to me, but they wouldn't have the law on their side.'

'Mrs Hammond has told us not to talk to anyone at all.'

'I assure you that you're doing nothing wrong. Presumably

29

you recognised Lumley as soon as he came into the shop that morning?'

'Yes. He was about a minute ahead of the others. He said something like, "Tell my uncle I'm here" and a few seconds later the other two burst in. One waved a gun about while the other smashed the showcase. Mr Hammond came out from the back room and the gun immediately went off. I let out a scream and fell to the floor and then it was all over.'

'Where was Mrs Hammond at the time?'

'I think she was still in the back room. I seem to remember her calling out something like, "Oh, do be careful, Bernard." Mr Hammond staggered back when the shot was fired and I saw Mrs Hammond supporting him. He was bleeding from his left shoulder and she was shouting, "Phone the police, phone the police".' She gave a small reflective smile. 'Philip – he's the other assistant – couldn't stop shaking. His mouth kept opening and closing, but no sound came out. I shouldn't really find it funny, except that Philip was always boasting about his macho qualities.'

Rosa was thoughtful for a moment. 'At the time it was happening did you associate Lumley with the robbery?'

The girl frowned. 'Well, he ran away with them, didn't he? Why did he do that if he wasn't one of the gang?'

'But he did nothing to arouse your suspicions when he first entered the shop?'

'No, though I remember thinking he looked a bit agitated.'

'Do you recall what he was doing while the robbery was taking place?'

'Not really. I think he just stood there.'

'But it definitely wasn't he who fired the shot?'

'No.'

'Or broke the showcase?'

'No.'

Rosa sighed. 'Well, I mustn't keep you talking. You've been most helpful and I promise I won't tell anyone about our meeting. Incidentally, do you happen to know Philip's address?'

'I think he shares a flat out at Acton with two or three other boys.'

'I'm not sure I even know his name . . . '

'Philip Wadingham. Do you think the police will catch the other two?' Susan asked, as she got up.

'I hope so. It would certainly be in Lumley's interest.'

Susan lowered her voice. 'It's rumoured that the police believe the robbers had inside information.'

'Have you heard any names mentioned?'

'There's a man called Fritz Dunster who is said to have a long-standing grudge against Mr Hammond.'

Rosa refrained from commenting that it was the same rumour that had reached the sandwich bar, where it was being attributed to Mrs Hammond. Whether or not that was significant remained to be seen.

Shortly afterwards the two women parted company, Rosa to take a Central Line westbound train to Notting Hill Gate, which was the station nearest to her flat on Campden Hill; Susan to take one in the opposite direction to Woodford.

As she reviewed her afternoon's work, she felt reasonably satisfied with what she had found out. Not that it left Stephen Lumley anywhere other than still in the centre of the frame.

Chapter 5

Rosa always missed Peter Chen when he was away. They had known each other for about three years and enjoyed a generally easy-going relationship. She was genuinely fond of him, but had been careful not to put him under emotional pressure. He had no such qualms and could change abruptly from a mood of sexual jealousy to one of tender passion.

Above all, however, they had become constant companions. Peter, with his infinitely more lucrative practice and with a string of wealthy clients, had always taken a lively and constructive interest in her cases.

Now he was back in Hong Kong for six months attending to complex family business. Admittedly he phoned Rosa regularly, but it wasn't the same thing as having him, so to speak, round the corner.

She would have especially welcomed being able to talk to him about Stephen Lumley's case. The telephone simply wasn't made for that sort of exchange.

Following her visit to Hammond's shop, she spent Sunday at home, cleaning her flat and preparing a case for court on Monday. Her thoughts, however, kept returning to Lumley.

She now knew that if he was to have any chance of acquittal, the defence would have to put up as many hares as possible. Fritz Dunster was, on the face of it, a putative hare, as would be anyone else with sufficient grudge against Hammond. Only that way might it be possible to sow seeds of doubt in a jury's mind about Stephen Lumley's extremely ambiguous behaviour.

From time to time, solicitors in criminal practice have need to use the services of a private inquiry agent, though Rosa preferred to avoid their employment if she could. In any event, the agent, to whose services she had had recourse on past occasions, had become hors de combat, after falling from a ladder while peeping into an upstairs bedroom in the course of duty.

Being loath to employ anyone new, she had on two recent occasions asked Ben, the firm's young and zestful all-purposes clerk, to undertake private inquiries on her behalf. He had readily agreed and had shown considerable initiative in achieving what was required of him. It had been rather like throwing a stick for an eager puppy. Also earning a bit of extra money never displeased him.

When, the next afternoon, she mentioned the matter to Robin Snaith, he simply said, 'I don't mind, if Ben doesn't and provided it doesn't interfere too greatly with his normal office duties.' He paused. 'Incidentally, is he growing a beard?'

'It's his designer stubble. His girlfriend prefers him that way to being smooth-cheeked.'

Robin ran a hand over his own face.

'Perhaps I ought to give my wife the option.'

Christine Lumley found her prison visits becoming an increasing strain. It wasn't simply that they involved a tiresome journey with several changes of bus and all for a mere fifteen minutes when she got there, but that often she left feeling more depressed and despairing than when she arrived.

Although she made the effort to go most days, she had begun to wonder if her visits were really worthwhile. Stephen was increasingly morose and on some days barely uttered half a dozen words.

And yet she knew that she would reproach herself if she made excuses for not going. And whatever his mood, he had never suggested she should cut down on her visits.

She now planned in advance what she was going to say

and so avoid painful silences. Even so there were days when she felt he had ceased to be the man she had married and with whom she was still in love.

But was it really surprising that what he was going through had wrought changes in him? The answer to that question was always 'no' and she knew that it was up to her to remain his lifeline.

'Max has drawn you a picture,' she said one afternoon in the week following Rosa's visit to Hammond's. She took a somewhat crumpled sheet of paper from her handbag.

'You've not told him where I am?' her husband said sharply.

'Of course, I haven't. They think you're in hospital. I tell them you're infectious and that's why they can't visit you.' As she spoke she glanced around the room which resembled a down-at-heel works' canteen. Wives and girlfriends sat talking to the men they had come to visit, some in furtive whispers, others at apparent ease, while kids chased each other noisily round the tables. She was thankful that Stephen didn't want to see Max and Cheryl under such conditions.

'You won't be able to keep up that pretence if I get sent down for ten years,' he said, with brutal frankness.

She gazed across the table at him with a mixture of fear and anger.

'I won't have you talk like that. You're innocent.'

He stared moodily around him.

'Ninety per cent of the poor sods awaiting trial here say they're innocent, but that won't prevent them being sent down by some crusty old judge.'

'You're talking daft,' she said vigorously. Reaching across the table she took his hand and fixed him with a steady look. With quiet emphasis she went on, 'Next time you see Miss Epton, I want you to tell her that you weren't running away from the shop, you were chasing the two men to stop *them* getting away. That's what really happened, wasn't it?'

He looked away and said nothing.

It was a thought that had been in her subconscious for some time and now she had given utterance to it. But why couldn't Stephen have reacted more positively? There were

34

times when she wondered if he was holding something back from her.

It was a few days later that Ben knocked on Rosa's door and entered with a well-pleased expression.

'You can forget all about Fritz Dunster, Miss E. The poor old boy has had a stroke and couldn't organise a game of tiddlywinks, let alone an armed robbery. He lives with his daughter and son-in-law out Edmonton way. Or rather they live with him, as it's his house. It was his wife's, but she died a year ago and he inherited.'

'You seem to have found out a great deal very quickly,' Rosa remarked in an admiring tone.

'There aren't all that many Dunsters in the telephone directory and I just phoned round the likely ones till I hit on Fritz.'

'But he mightn't have been living in London at all, or for that matter, been a telephone subscriber,' Rosa said with a touch of legal fastidiousness.

'Then it would have taken longer,' Ben replied airily. 'Anyway, I went out to Edmonton last night and visited him. He's our chap all right. He'd read about the robbery at Hammond's. It had cheered him up no end, particularly that Bernard Hammond got a bullet through his shoulder. Said it should have been through his heart.'

'His stroke hasn't affected him that badly then?'

'He's in a wheel-chair, but his speech is reasonably OK. Also his mind does a bit of free-wheeling, but he remembers Hammond as though he were today's bad news. He used to do a lot of jewellery repair work for the firm on a freelance basis. Then Bernard Hammond lent him money to enlarge his own business, only to pull the mat from under him when the going got a bit tough. Dunster had to sell everything at a loss and was left ruined.'

'How long ago was all this?'

'A couple of years. It was as a direct result that he had his stroke.' Ben looked thoughtful. 'I think my visit cheered him up.'

'What excuse did you give for calling on him?'

'Said I was a freelance reporter writing a piece about the robbery for when the case was over and was researching the background.'

'And he swallowed that?'

'Of course. Why shouldn't he have? He was eager to talk. He still hates Bernard Hammond's guts.'

'Did he say whether the police had been to see him?'

'He said a young constable had been to the house, taken a quick look at him and gone away again. I imagine the police have now crossed him off their list.'

'I suppose it must have been Mrs Hammond who put him in the first place,' Rosa observed thoughtfully.

'If she put the police on to him, she can't have seen him recently.' He gave Rosa a hopeful look. 'Anyone else you want running to earth?'

'Not at the moment, Ben. I must try and get hold of a list of Hammond's employees over the past two years. There may be others with strong grudges against their ex-employer.'

'Like me to investigate that angle for you?' he asked eagerly.

'Possibly later. Even, probably later. But first I'll wait till I've received the prosecution's statements and seen the strength of the case we have to meet.'

'Do you think our chap's innocent?'

'All I know is that, if he is innocent, he's the most hapless victim of circumstances I've ever come across. And to accept that goes against my instinct . . .' Her voice trailed away.

Ben grinned. Observing Miss E could be like watching a weather vane on a breezy day.

Chapter 6

It was four weeks to the day after the robbery took place that Rosa received the bundle of prosecution statements.

She found them sitting on her desk when she returned from court one afternoon and immediately put everything else on one side to give them a preliminary read. It wasn't a large bundle, but then it wasn't a particularly complicated case from the prosecution's point of view. Three men had robbed a jeweller's shop, two had got away and the third caught as near red-handed as made no difference. It was as simple as that.

She riffled through the bundle before turning to Bernard Hammond's statement.

Giving an address in Highgate and his age as sixty-two, he went on:

> I am a jeweller by occupation and am the owner of Bernard Hammond and Co in Firley Street, W1 where I have traded for the past twenty-five years. I am assisted in the running of the business by my wife, who does all the secretarial work. I also employ two sales persons in the shop, Philip Wadingham and Susan Cunliffe.
>
> Mine is a high-class business and I hold a great deal of valuable stock on my premises. I am fully insured.
>
> I have a nephew named Stephen Lumley who is the son of my deceased sister, Jean. On a number of occasions I have helped Stephen financially, but last July we had a row and I told him to keep away as I was not prepared to help him further. Stephen became

aggressive and said I would live to regret it. I asked him if he was trying to threaten me and he said I'd find out in due time. I told him to get out and stay out of my life. This all happened one evening at my home after he'd arrived without warning.

I next saw Stephen on the day of the robbery which was Wednesday, 28th October. It was around half past eleven in the morning and I was in the back room which I use as an office. My wife was there, too. I suddenly heard the sound of breaking glass in the shop and went to see what was happening. A curtain hangs across the dividing doorway. As I pulled it aside, I saw three men in a row on the other side of the counter. One of them was my nephew, Stephen Lumley. Almost immediately a shot was fired and I was hit in my left shoulder. I staggered back and fell to the floor and my wife began screaming. I didn't notice where Susan Cunliffe and Philip Wadingham were. I was only aware of the three men. After the shot was fired, they turned and dashed out of the shop. Two of the men (not Lumley) had large black moustaches and were wearing hats. I can't tell you anything more about them. I'm sure I would recognise them again if their appearance remained unchanged, though with the benefit of hindsight, it's my belief they were wearing wigs and false moustaches. Stephen Lumley was not wearing any form of disguise. Later I was taken to hospital where the bullet was removed from my shoulder. I have made a good recovery, but am still undergoing physiotherapy for my damaged shoulder muscles.

The robbers got away with jewellery to the value of about £100,000, mostly diamond and sapphire rings and some pearl necklaces.

As to who fired the shot, it was either Lumley or the man next to him. I can't say which.

I haven't any doubt in my own mind that Stephen Lumley was acting in concert with the other two men.

Normally an alarm bell should have gone off when the glass in the showcase was broken, but there was a short-circuit in the system which an electrician was coming to repair later that day.

I have read this statement and it is true.

It was clear to Rosa that the statement had been obtained in answer to police questions. Most witnesses' statements were obtained that way. It led to a tidy, well-trimmed narrative containing the essence of what was needed to prove the charge.

As Rosa glanced again at the last few sentences, she could hear an officer smoothly ask, 'Did you get the impression that Lumley was acting in concert with the other two?' By then the police would have interrogated Lumley and would know that he denied participation in the robbery.

The next statement she turned to was that of Carol Hammond, who gave the same Highgate address and her age as thirty-six. She went on to say that she did all the secretarial work in the business and helped out on the counter when required.

On Wednesday, 28th October, I was in the office at the rear of the shop when I heard the sound of breaking glass. It was about half past eleven in the morning. My husband immediately moved towards the doorway leading into the shop. I called out to him to be careful. Suddenly a shot rang out and my husband spun round and fell to the floor. I screamed for help and went to him. I thought he might have been killed.

I never saw the robbers myself. My first concern was for my husband and I didn't look into the shop. I know my husband's nephew Stephen Lumley, but wasn't aware he'd been in the shop until I was told he had been arrested on the pavement while he was trying to escape. I know that he had threatened my husband after my husband refused to lend him more money.

That is all I can tell you.

Apart from the bit of venom in the penultimate sentence, it was a restrained, even self-effacing, statement. As to Lumley having threatened her husband, Rosa had little doubt it had been elicited by a direct question. Though her evidence wasn't immaterial, the prosecution could manage perfectly well without it. Maybe the police were hoping that the defence would give her an opportunity to put the boot in when it came to the trial.

She turned to Susan Cunliffe's statement which was in line with what she had told Rosa when they talked, though with a number of subtle differences. She laid emphasis on the fact that Lumley seemed extremely nervous when he entered the shop. There was a clear implication that he knew the robbery was about to take place. She said he had asked her to tell his uncle that he would like to speak to him.

Rosa pondered the statement in the light of what DI Cleave had suggested, namely that Lumley's rôle had been that of decoy. But a decoy to what purpose, she asked herself? If he was there to distract the counter staff before the other two burst in and got on with the robbery, surely it would have been more sensible for him to remain when they fled? After all, he was known in the shop and by not running away he would have enhanced his own credibility, something which headlong flight had singularly failed to achieve.

In the words of the Epistle, she felt she was seeing through a glass, darkly. She hoped enlightenment would come later.

Philip Wadingham had not been in the shop the Saturday afternoon she made her visit and she turned to his statement with interest, recalling what Susan had said about his not-so-heroic behaviour.

He was twenty-nine and described himself as a gemmologist. Rosa doubted, however, whether he held the diploma to justify that description. He stated that around ten o'clock on the morning of Wednesday, 28th October, when Mr and Mrs Hammond were otherwise engaged, he had answered the phone in the office. The caller sounded tense and he, the witness, got the impression he was trying to disguise his voice. He wanted to know whether Mr Hammond was in that morning. He declined to give his name or leave a message and abruptly rang off. The witness now believed the caller had been Mr Hammond's nephew, Stephen Lumley, though he hadn't placed him at the time.

Some time around half past eleven, he had been at the further end of the counter from Susan Cunliffe, wrapping a gold chain which a customer was due to pick up. He heard the shop door open and looked up to see Lumley enter.

I thought he looked extremely nervous, even furtive, and I wondered why. I saw him approach Miss Cunliffe and say something to her which I didn't hear. Almost immediately two more men came in. I was struck by their appearance. They had heavy moustaches and long hair and were wearing hats. As I got ready to serve them, one of them produced a hammer and smashed the glass in the showcase while the other threatened me with a revolver. When I say threatened, I mean he pointed it straight at me. I heard Mr Hammond say something from the office doorway and immediately a shot rang out. I dropped to the ground and started to crawl towards Mr Hammond who was bleeding badly. Mrs Hammond was having hysterics and Miss Cunliffe was too shocked to do anything, so it was up to me to take charge.

I am almost certain that the man who had the revolver said something to Lumley just before the shot was fired. I didn't hear what he said, but I got the impression that they weren't strangers to each other.

Rosa underlined this last sentence. In due course she would annotate all the statements and hand them to Lumley for his own comments.

There were the usual statements of police evidence and others relating to the scientific examination of the shop premises and of the bullet removed from Bernard Hammond's shoulder, but none of these interested her at the moment.

Leafing back, she turned her attention to the statement of Alistair Yates of Flat six, thirty-four Firley Street, who

41

described himself as a company director and told how, on Wednesday, 28th October, he was walking along the pavement on his way to his local pub for a lunch-time drink when he heard a muffled shot and saw three men burst from Hammond's, the jewellers. Two of them leapt into a Jaguar car which was double-parked outside and which drove off at high speed. The third man seemed to dither for a moment before

> pelting down the pavement in my direction. I put out my foot and tripped him up. Then I sat on him until the police came. He put up no resistance. I weigh eighteen stone and played rugby football until last year when I dislocated my shoulder.
>
> When I say that the man I tripped seemed to dither for a moment, I mean that he appeared to hesitate about joining the others in the getaway car.

Rosa sighed. The taking of statements was, indeed, an art form.

She glanced at one of the police statements which told her that the car in which they had fled had been found abandoned half a mile away. It had been stolen a week previously and fitted with false plates.

She leaned back in her chair and stared in thought at the ceiling. It was apparent that the police had firmly committed themselves to securing the conviction of the one man they *had* caught.

Suddenly her phone rang and she lifted the receiver.

'It's Detective Inspector Cleave, Miss Epton. I just wanted to check that you got the statements in Lumley?'

'They arrived today.'

'Good. The CPS assured me they'd been sent, but I thought I'd just check.' He paused. 'Have you had a chance to look at them yet?'

'As a matter of fact, I've just been giving them a preliminary once-over.'

'Then you'll have seen what I meant about Lumley doing himself a favour by telling us the names of the other two. I can't believe he wants to take the full rap. If he'll help us, I'm sure we'll be able to help him. We accept that he wasn't personally armed, even if there's an obvious inference that he was a party to the use of a gun.' Cleave paused and added in a honeyed tone, 'But it's not an irresistible inference, if you take my meaning; though it could make quite a difference to the sentence he gets.'

'I take your meaning very well, Mr Cleave,' Rosa observed in a dry tone.

What it amounted to was that the police would soft-pedal their evidence against Lumley on that particular point if he helped them make further arrests. But how could he help them if he didn't know who the men were? It would be a cruel enough dilemma if he was aware of their identities. It was a truly diabolical situation, if he was telling the truth.

Chapter 7

'How am I ever going to get out of this?' Lumley said
despairingly. 'Everything's been twisted against me.'

He and Rosa faced each other in one of the small interview-
rooms reserved for lawyers visiting their incarcerated clients.
She had intended leaving him the bundle of statements to
read at his leisure – unoccupied time was the one thing in
abundance for most prisoners – but he had insisted on going
through them with her there and then and she hadn't the
heart to refuse him.

'There are points in your favour as well as against you,'
Rosa said. 'On the credit side is the fact you entered the
shop independently, weren't wearing any sort of disguise
and asked to speak to your uncle. Also that, apart from
your physical proximity to the robbers, you played no part
in either the shooting or the theft of jewellery. The strongest
evidence against you is that you ran away with the others and
the prosecution will certainly invite a jury to draw an implication of guilt from that. They will, of course, also say you
had a motive, but I don't believe that will bear too close an
examination. It doesn't seem to me very credible to suggest
that you either took part for gain or as an act of revenge.'

Lumley gave an abstracted nod, then, with a thoughtful
look, said, 'Supposing I were to say I was really chasing
them when they fled the shop, that I was hoping to prevent
their escape?'

Rosa stared at him uncertainly while deciding how best
to bring down this forlorn kite.

'You would be asked why, if that was your intention,

you had subsequently dashed off along the pavement. Why hadn't you gone back into the shop and said, "Sorry, Uncle, I'm afraid they got away," or something to that effect? Prosecuting counsel could give you a very uncomfortable time.'

He glowered. 'If I was part of the raid, why didn't I escape in the car with the others? Answer me that!'

'It's certainly a point we'll make. I anticipate, however, that the prosecution will say you had a diversionary rôle. That's why you entered ahead of the others and weren't wearing a disguise.'

'That's rubbish.'

'We have to persuade the jury it's rubbish.'

'But I'm innocent,' he exclaimed in anguish.

'The police believe you could tell them the names of the other two.'

'How many more times do I have to say I don't know? Even if my life depended on it, I couldn't help. And that's still the truth, Miss Epton.' In a calmer voice, he went on, 'So what happens now?'

'You'll be committed for trial at the Old Bailey. It would be a waste of time and energy to contest the case in the magistrates' court. Much best to conserve our strength for the trial.'

'Meanwhile I have to languish in prison?'

'I'm afraid so.'

'Even though I'm innocent?' he said bitterly.

'Yes.'

'I thought British justice was meant to be the best in the world.'

'That doesn't mean it's perfect.'

'You can't spend a few weeks in the Scrubs without finding that out.'

Or in a solicitor's office, Rosa felt inclined to say, but didn't.

'How's your wife bearing up?' she asked in a sympathetic tone.

'Not well. The strain's getting her down and I'm no help when she visits me. I get all tight inside and can't talk to her any more. Anyway, there's nothing to say. We've run out of conversation. At least, I have.'

Rosa was only too well aware of the intolerable pressures that prison placed on a marriage. And for Lumley, it was still only the beginning . . .

'I'll let the court know that we'll accept a paper committal. Once that's over I can get down to briefing counsel and preparing your defence.'

'You better brief a magician. I'll need one.'

'I'll brief a capable, competent barrister. They're more predictable than magicians. Meanwhile, read the statements carefully and make a note of anything that occurs to you. I'll see you at court next week.'

As she drove back to her office, she reflected on her visit. She decided that it was his artlessness, as well as his sense of deep despair, which persuaded her he wasn't play-acting the rôle of the innocent. He had never said anything to give her cause to doubt his word. Anything, that is, beyond the basic improbability of an outrageous coincidence.

And if he was innocent, then fate, for her own perverse reasons, had not only decided to knock him down, but to put the heavy boot in as well.

'Is it the same old buzzard as last time?' Lumley enquired of Rosa when they met at the magistrates' court the following week.

'It's the same magistrate, if that's what you mean,' Rosa replied. She didn't dissent from the description, but felt a certain obligation not to traduce the magistracy on its own territory. 'Anyway, he'll have nothing to do save commit you for trial, so you won't be dependent on him for any favours. I ought to warn you that the clerk of the court will read you a notice about alibi evidence. He's required to do that by law, but it has no application in your case as you won't be putting up an alibi defence.'

'Wish I could.'

'In my experience, alibis can all too easily backfire and then you're really sunk.'

'I still wouldn't mind having a watertight one at the moment,' he said wistfully.

'When the case is called on, leave everything to me. I'll do whatever talking is necessary, including applying for legal aid.'

'And bail?'

'That's still a non-starter.'

'There was a bloke in the Scrubs who got bail on a robbery charge.'

'It wouldn't have been an armed robbery. The use of a gun puts you firmly on the wrong side of the bail line. OK, I know you weren't carrying a weapon, but that's what the charge against you involves.'

As soon as Rosa had taken her seat in court, the clerk leaned forward and said, 'I gather Lumley's a Section 6 (2) committal?'

'Yes.'

'Excellent. I take it you're not applying for bail, but would like legal aid?'

'Correct both times.'

'No problems then,' he said, giving her a relieved smile.

The magistrate, meanwhile, was listening with signs of restlessness to a probation officer's report. He had little respect for probation, though it was often a convenient way of getting rid of a case.

Eventually the probation officer departed from the witness-box and the jailer announced, 'Remand number two, your worship. Stephen Lumley.'

'Miss Epton represents the defendant, sir and is agreeable to a Section 6 (2) committal,' the clerk said, addressing the magistrate. 'Mr Ive appears on behalf of the CPS.'

A thin, pale young man half-rose and acknowledged his presence.

'I haven't got any papers with me,' he hissed at Rosa. 'But I don't suppose it matters. I wasn't told the case was coming on today.'

'You can look at mine if you want,' Rosa said obligingly.

47

'Thanks.' With a sigh, he added, 'With luck we'll sort ourselves out one day.'

A few minutes later Lumley had been committed in custody to stand his trial at the Central Criminal Court, otherwise known as the Old Bailey. He had also been granted legal aid for one counsel.

DI Cleave was waiting for Rosa as she came out of court.

'Superintendent Forrester has asked me to have a word with you, Miss Epton,' he said with a small, hopeful smile.

'On the same matter as before?'

'On whether your client has had a change of mind about helping the police.'

Rosa let out a sigh. 'That's what I thought you meant. He still insists that he played no part in the robbery and has no idea who the robbers were.'

'Mr Forrester is most anxious to make further arrests and clear the matter up,' he said in a pressing tone.

'Lumley is absolutely adamant that he wasn't involved.'

'You don't actually believe that yourself, do you, Miss Epton?'

'Since you ask, yes, I believe he's innocent.'

'Innocent?' Cleave echoed incredulously. He stared at Rosa as though looking for a sign that she was having him on.

'Incidentally,' Rosa went on, 'if you're thinking of trying to see him in prison between now and his trial, save your energy. You'll be wasting your time.'

Cleave shrugged. 'Well, let me know if he has a change of mind.'

'Has it not occurred to you that you may have charged an innocent person?' Rosa asked tartly.

'Only two sorts of people find their way into the dock of the Old Bailey, Miss Epton. Those who are guilty and who get sent down; and those who are guilty, but manage to get off.'

'And I always thought you were an enlightened officer.'

'I hope I am, but that doesn't mean I'm also soft-headed.'

As he turned to go, Rosa went on, 'You say that Super-intendent Forrester is anxious to clear the case up. For him, however, it's merely a matter of professional pride and of a tidy set of statistics. For my client it's a question of survival or destruction as an individual.'

'You're a good advocate, Miss Epton,' he said. Then in a more serious tone, he went on, 'Perhaps you will believe me when I tell you that the thought of a genuinely innocent person having to fight against odds for his liberty fills me with dismay and horror. Fortunately, to the best of my belief, I've never been involved in such a case.'

'There has to be a first time for everything,' Rosa remarked with a tight smile.

Chapter 8

Like the mills of God, those of criminal justice grind slowly, though with less exactness.

Rosa knew it would be six months or more before Stephen Lumley was tried. In the meantime he would have to endure his incarceration, with all too little to sustain his morale.

After his committal for trial, he was transferred to Brixton Prison which meant a longer and more difficult journey for his wife. She no longer attempted to visit him every day. Apart from anything else, she couldn't afford the fare more than twice a week. As she strove to keep her home going, she almost certainly suffered more than her husband. She was anxious that the children shouldn't forget their father, while, at the same time, not wishing constantly to remind them of his absence. Fortunately, they seemed willing to accept that he was still ill.

'Some people,' she told them, 'have to stay in hospital a very long time.'

'Has he got Aids?' Max enquired on his return from school one afternoon.

It seemed that a boy in his form – there's always at least one of the precocious kind – had said that Aids was the only illness to keep you in hospital so long. Fortunately, he hadn't imparted any further knowledge of the disease, if indeed he possessed it, and Max didn't show any interest in his father's clinical symptoms. His only comment was that it was a funny name for an illness.

Rosa, for her part, made a point of visiting Lumley in prison at least once a month, which was more than strict duty required. He seemed to appreciate her visits as evidence that he wasn't a forgotten man.

She was able to tell him that she had briefed Paul Maxted for the defence and would be discussing the case with him as soon as he had read the papers she had sent him. She didn't mention that counsel were generally disinclined to read their briefs until closer to the date of trial and she had made a special plea to Maxted's clerk for an early conference.

She also kept in touch with Christine Lumley and did what little she could to buoy up her spirits. As far as she was able to make out, there was no immediate threat to the marriage, though once or twice when they were talking she gained the impression that Christine had contingency plans in mind should her husband be convicted. She no longer spoke of his innocence in such an insistent manner. The irony of this was not lost on Rosa.

Paul Maxted, whom Rosa frequently briefed, was in his late thirties and had Chambers in Mulberry Court in the Temple. He was a genial, unflappable individual who always fought hard for his clients. Judges respected him and he was held in popular esteem by his fellow counsel. He and Rosa got on well and enjoyed a close professional relationship.

It was a late afternoon in mid-January when Rosa went along to his Chambers for a conference.

'Gather you wanted an early con in this case, Rosa,' he said after he had welcomed her and they were seated. 'Hence, I've read the papers rather sooner than I might have done. Can't see it coming to trial for a few months yet. It was only committed in December and the waiting-list at the Bailey doesn't seem to get any shorter. Anyway, what's the particular problem?'

'I believe Lumley's innocent,' Rosa said, meeting counsel's gaze.

Paul Maxted's expression gave nothing away. He was used to hiding his feelings, save when he wished otherwise. For the benefit of a jury, for example.

'I confess it hadn't occurred to me that he might be innocent, despite his protestations,' he said slowly. 'I'm not saying he doesn't have a run for his money, though I wouldn't personally want to bet on his chances. He's got some very awkward corners to negotiate in his evidence.'

Rosa nodded. 'I know. That's what makes it worse believing he's innocent.'

'I agree that it always makes defending that much more onerous. On the whole I've trained myself never to think in terms of innocence, only of unproven guilt within the rules of evidence.' He paused. 'What in particular has persuaded you of his innocence?'

Rosa gave a helpless shrug. 'It's simply an impression that's grown more solid with time. He strikes me as a straightforward person without any artifice and I've not once had reason to think he was being devious with me.'

'I see. Of course I've not yet met him, but he has certainly landed himself in one hell of a fix.'

'I know. I'm sorry to have burdened you with my personal feelings about the case, but I owe it to Lumley to do so.'

'Absolutely. I take it you're not likely to change your mind about him?'

'I can't think why I should.'

'Nor can I, unless there are further developments between now and trial.'

'Such as the arrest of the other two, you mean?'

'Exactly. If that happened, we could find ourselves in a completely different ball game. Supposing, for example, they claimed that Lumley was in it from the beginning; that it was he who planned it, etcetera.'

'I wouldn't believe them.'

'Supposing,' Maxted went on, 'Lumley held up his hand and said, "Yes, it's true"?'

'He won't. He has nothing to fear from the arrest of the other two. He wants it.'

'We talk about the other two, but it's probably three, isn't it? The getaway car had a driver waiting at the wheel, even though nobody seems to have noticed him.' He was thoughtful for a while. 'If, and I repeat if,' he went on in a reflective tone, 'Lumley had nothing to do with the robbery, it would be interesting to know how Hammond's shop came to be picked on? The prosecution, of course, is going to say "Look no further than the penniless, grudge-bearing nephew", but I agree with you that to say that begs more questions than it answers. Let's suppose that Lumley is, as you believe, quite innocent, then who was behind the robbery? Somebody must have been. Armed robbers don't just pick their victims' names out of a hat. Somebody has to say, "Look boys, I know a good place for some easy pickings, Bernard Hammond's jewellery shop in Firley Street." Moreover, that somebody invariably has inside knowledge.'

'I know,' Rosa said keenly. 'I've been making enquiries about disgruntled employees and the like, but so far without finding any worthwhile scent.'

'You mention a Fritz Dunster in the brief . . . '

'He certainly had a vengeance motive against Hammond, but he'd have been physically incapable of organising the robbery.'

Maxted pursed his lips. 'People in wheel-chairs have been known to mastermind crimes.' He gave Rosa a self-deprecating smile. 'But perhaps I watch too much TV.'

'There is someone else I'm hoping to find out more about. A Leslie Fingle who used to work at Hammond's and got the sack for embezzlement. That was about two years ago. Since then he appears to have been drifting. He's into drugs and that, as we both know, costs money.'

'Where does he hang out?'

'He was in Brighton until recently.'

'How'd you find out about him?'

'Through Ben, our general clerk, who also doubles as a private eye on occasions,' Rosa said with a smile. 'Anyway, Fingle is still in Ben's sights.'

'I inferred from what you said that he had disappeared.'

'He's not frequenting his usual haunts, but Ben is hopeful of tracing him. What then remains to be seen.'

Paul Maxted leaned back in his chair and stretched out his arms.

'Once the trial date has been set, we'd better have another

con and review our tactics.' He gave Rosa a rueful look. 'Meanwhile, I'm bound to say I think the prosecution has a compelling case.'

That was mid-January and it was early June before R v. Lumley was listed to come before His Honour Judge Grapham, one of the Old Bailey's most senior and experienced permanent judges. Though generally regarded as being firmly pro-police and pro-prosecution, there were occasions when he was capable of swinging completely the other way if the defence managed to overcome the natural odds and win his support.

Chapter 9

Stephen Lumley stepped into the dock of court number eight and looked about him with the wariness of an animal suspicious of its new habitat.

Rosa gave him a quick smile, but he appeared not to notice her in the sea of faces. In the court's artificial light the underlying copper tones of his hair showed up.

Rosa and Paul Maxted had visited him in the cells beneath the court to have a last word before the case began. They had found him uptight and nervous at the ordeal ahead. He was wearing his one and only suit (sage green) with a shirt and tie. On Rosa's recommendation, his wife had taken it to him in prison and told him he was to wear it at his trial.

'Miss Epton says it's important that you look neat and tidy,' she had said when handing it over. 'And you certainly can't wear what you were arrested in. A windcheater and T-shirt are a complete giveaway.'

'What's that supposed to mean?' he asked mutinously.

She bit her lip. 'You know I didn't mean it as a jibe. But promise me you will wear it,' she said in a coaxing tone.

'I promise.'

'I love you so much, Steve,' she said with a slight gulp.

'Now, don't go all soft. After all, you may soon be looking for a new husband.'

It had not been one of her better visits.

Lumley continued to gaze around the court, at counsel in their wigs and gowns nonchalantly waiting for the trial to begin, at the clerk of the court standing up with his back to everyone as he held a whispered conversation with the judge.

The clerk suddenly sat down and Judge Grapham and Stephen Lumley found themselves staring at each other. The judge's gaze was one of remote indifference. Defendants passed through his court with the regularity of rain clouds across an English sky and he would seldom recognise any of them again. His mind at the present moment was more on the golf competition in which he was due to play at the weekend than on the case that was about to begin. After five days spent in court (and this was Friday) he always looked forward to his weekend golf. He was a tall, thin man with a deep voice.

The clerk now read out the indictment which contained counts of robbery and wounding with intent to cause grievous bodily harm, replacing the attempted murder charge, to both of which Lumley pleaded not guilty in a tense voice. Rosa knew that if the police had had their way, there would have been more than two counts. They always believed in overkill when it came to charges.

Next came the empanelling of the jury which Lumley watched with anxious care. These were the men and women who would eventually decide his fate. He blinked in surprise when his counsel sprang up and challenged a middle-aged Indian who was thereupon requested by the judge to leave the jury-box. Appearing stunned and aggrieved the hapless man made his way out of court.

'Prosperous-looking Indians usually mean shopkeepers,' Paul Maxted whispered to Rosa, 'and we don't want any of them on the jury.'

When finally sworn, the jury comprised five women and seven men. Three of the women were plump, motherly types (one of them black), one had the earnest, slightly harassed expression of a voluntary social worker and the fifth was a smartly dressed executive type. Five of the men were in their late thirties or early forties and looked like steady, law-abiding citizens, which didn't, of course, mean that they were. One was a young man of impassive oriental appearance and the last was a youth with streaked hair who was dressed largely in black leather. The judge had eyed him suspiciously as he took the oath, but the youth had appeared relaxed and immediately afterwards had whispered something to the motherly lady next to him who gave him a warm smile.

The clerk of the court read out the indictment, told the jury that the defendant had pleaded not guilty and that they should accordingly harken unto the evidence.

'Yes, Mr Hobden,' Judge Grapham said, glancing at prosecuting counsel with the resigned air he invariably brought to each new case. He might have been an actor in *The Mousetrap* who hadn't missed a single performance in thirty-five years.

Oliver Hobden was one of Treasury Counsel at the Old Bailey who undertook the more serious prosecutions. He was a competent and extremely hardworking advocate.

'May it please your lordship, members of the jury, in this case I appear for the crown and the defendant is represented by my learned friend, Mr Maxted.

'On 28th October last year, around eleven thirty in the morning, three men entered Bernard Hammond and Co, a jeweller's shop in Firley Street, W1. One of the three was the defendant, Lumley, who is the nephew of the shop owner, Mr Bernard Hammond ... ' Counsel went on to give a factual account of what took place and then said, 'Two of the men made good their escape and have never been traced. That, however, need not prevent you from convicting this defendant if the evidence satisfies you that he participated in the robbery. The fact that it wasn't he who fired the gun or wielded the hammer doesn't mean that he can't be found guilty if the crown proves beyond reasonable doubt that he was a party to what took place and that this was a joint enterprise by all three men ... ' He glanced down at his notebook and turned a page. 'There is one particular matter I should mention to you before calling the evidence. You may well be asking yourselves why should two of the men have been wearing disguises, but not this defendant?' If the jury was indeed asking itself such a question, its corporate expression gave nothing away. Counsel went on,

'The answer is not hard to find, for the prosecution suggests you may properly infer from the evidence that it was this defendant who initiated the robbery, being the person with inside knowledge of Hammond's business. His arrival at the shop a minute or so ahead of the other two was intended as a diversionary tactic to deflect attention from their own entry.' He paused and gave his gown a hitch. 'Lumley, of course, denies having anything to do with the robbery and says that his presence in the shop when it took place was a pure coincidence.' He gave the jury a stern look. 'If you are inclined to accept such a preposterous explanation, let me remind you that the defendant had a potent motive for the crime. A double motive, indeed. Revenge and financial gain.'

A few minutes later, Hobden concluded his opening and said that he would now call his evidence. A plan showing a stretch of Firley Street and a lay-out of the interior of Hammond's shop was produced by way of a certificate from its draughtsman. There was also an album of photographs showing the same details as the plan, with the addition of a photo of the shoulder wound sustained by Uncle Bernard.

The jury, relieved at being able to do something other than listen, seized on copies of the two exhibits as if they were unexpected birthday presents.

The judge watched them with strained patience for a moment or two before remarking, 'Now that you've had a preliminary look at those two exhibits, I suggest you place them on the ledge in front of you until the evidence requires you to refer to them.'

'I call Bernard Hammond,' Hobden said, squaring his shoulders as if for a fight.

It was Rosa's first sight of Uncle Bernard and she watched his progress across the court to the witness-box. He was a short, sturdy man with a shiny bald head fringed by hair the colour of thick-cut marmalade. He was wearing a black jacket and striped trousers as though off to visit a wealthy client in a hotel suite.

His evidence followed the lines of his statement, though his attitude towards his nephew appeared to have hardened.

'What sort of terms were you on with the defendant?' Hobden enquired, his expression one of innocent interest.

'You mean latterly?'

'At the time of the robbery?'

'Bad terms as far as I was concerned.'

'Please explain.'

'My nephew had frequently come to me asking for loans, but last July I told him I was fed up with his constant pleas for cash and I wasn't going to lend him any more. He immediately flew into a temper and called me names and I told him to get out and stay out of my life. He then left my home after issuing threats.'

'What sort of threats?'

'He said I'd live to regret my refusal to help him and that he would get even with me.'

'What did you think he meant by that?'

'That he was bent on revenge; though I never actually thought he would go as far as he did.'

Prosecuting counsel sat down and Paul Maxted rose to cross-examine.

'I take your last answer, Mr Hammond, to mean that you never expected him to rob you?'

The witness hesitated a moment. 'No, I didn't, but I was obviously wrong.'

'You're aware that Lumley has, from the outset, denied being a participant in the robbery?'

'I'm afraid actions speak louder than words.'

'When you heard the sound of breaking glass in the shop and went to investigate, what exactly was Lumley doing?'

'He was standing beside the other two.'

'Merely standing?'

'I've already explained that I was shot almost as soon as I appeared in the connecting doorway. I certainly didn't have time to gaze around and take in the whole scene.'

'I understand perfectly,' Maxted said in smooth tone. 'Do you now accept that the shot was fired by the person standing between Lumley and the man with the hammer?'

'That's what I've been told,' the witness replied grudgingly.

'But you do accept it?'

'I've already said I didn't have time to see who fired the shot.'

'In your original statement to the police, you suggested it might have been Lumley ... '

'It could have been.'

'But do you now accept that it wasn't?'

'It's not for me to say.'

'You didn't have any reservations about naming the defendant in the first instance, did you?'

'I'm not sure what you're suggesting ... '

'What I'm suggesting, Mr Hammond, is that you wanted to believe it was your nephew who shot at you.' The witness glared at counsel who went on, 'It fitted in with your theory that he was after revenge.'

'It wasn't a theory,' Hammond said indignantly. 'He had threatened me.'

'In a fit of annoyance when you refused to lend him further money?'

'It was anger more than annoyance.'

'All of three months before the robbery took place?'

'Yes.'

'Come, Mr Hammond, you never took his threat seriously, did you? People often make idle threats when they're upset, don't they?'

'All I'm saying is that Stephen threatened me and later took part in the robbery.'

'In your view, the two events hang together?'

'Yes.'

'Were you utterly surprised to discover he was the member of an armed gang?'

'I'm still shocked.'

'It was the last thing you'd have expected?'

'Yes.'

'Supposing it had been one of your regular customers standing at the counter in the manner Lumley was standing, would you have assumed he was a member of the gang?'

'I can't answer such a hypothetical question.'

'Try.'

'Not necessarily.'

'And yet you immediately assumed Lumley was?'

'Yes, because . . . ' His voice tailed away.

'Because you automatically connected his presence with the threats he'd uttered several months before?'

'It was natural that I should.'

Maxted gave a quick satisfied nod. He had been keeping a watchful eye on the jury, who appeared to have followed the cross-examination with considerable attention. He turned to whisper something to Rosa before again confronting the witness.

'There's just one other matter I want to ask you about, Mr Hammond. Did you once employ a man named Leslie Fingle?'

The witness started in surprise. 'Yes, I did,' he said suspiciously.

'What name was that, Mr Maxted?' the judge broke in.

'Fingle, my lord. F–I–N–G–L–E.'

'Is he somebody we're likely to hear more of?'

'I'm not really sure, my lord.'

Judge Grapham turned to the witness.

'You once employed a man of that name, is that correct?'

'Yes, sir.'

'And what happened to him?'

'I dismissed him for dishonesty.'

'Have you had anything further to do with him since he left your employ?'

'No.'

'Has he ever uttered any threats against you?'

'No, sir. I'm not clear why his name has come up.'

'I don't think any of us are,' the judge remarked acidly.

A few minutes later Bernard Hammond was replaced in the witness-box by his wife. She was wearing a red and black check suit with a white blouse and looked as if she had come straight from the hairdresser.

As Hobden elicited her evidence, Rosa formed the im
pression she didn't wish to say anything that might provol
vigorous cross-examination. She emphasised the fact that sh
hadn't seen the faces of the men involved in the robbery an
couldn't really say very much to assist the court. She stressec
that she had been far too anxious about her wounded husband
to pay attention to anything else.

'How long have you been married, Mrs Hammond?'
Maxted asked as his opening question.

'About eighteen months,' she replied in obvious surprise.

'I believe you are Mr Hammond's third wife?'

'Yes.' Her tone became frigid. 'If you want to know, we
got married in December the year before last, following the
death of Mr Hammond's previous wife.'

'I believe you had worked in the shop for some years
before your marriage?'

'Yes.'

'Tell me, were you on good terms with the defendant
and his wife?'

The witness frowned. 'We were never close socially. As
far as I was concerned, Stephen was my husband's nephew
and that was it.'

'Were you surprised to learn that he'd been charged with
the robbery?'

She gave defending counsel a small superior smile. 'I take
it you mean, was I surprised he took part in the robbery? The
answer is that I was. Indeed, I was shattered. It's been a very
bitter experience for both my husband and myself.'

'You know that Lumley has all along denied playing any
part in the robbery?'

'I'm aware of that,' she said in a scornful tone.

'And as far as your direct knowledge is concerned, it
could be true?'

'My *direct* knowledge?' she said warily.

'What you yourself saw and heard at the time of the
robbery?'

'I've already explained, I didn't see anything as I was
in the office.'

'And all you heard was the sound of bre
of a shot being fired?'
'Yes, but I have no reason to doubt wha
told by others . . . '
'Maybe not, Mrs Hammond, but that's wh
hearsay evidence and isn't admissible in this cou

Carol Hammond gave a shrug to indicate sh
be held responsible for the caprices of British justi
while, Paul Maxted resumed his seat.

Next into the witness-box was Susan Cunliffe.
dence adhered faithfully to her written statement.
plainly nervous and turned to bolt from the court a
as prosecuting counsel completed his examination-in-

'I'm afraid I also have a few questions to ask you,
Cunliffe,' Maxted said in a not unfriendly tone. 'From
time the defendant entered the shop to the time he
did he do or say anything that suggested he was part of
robbery?'

'No, not exactly.'

'You assumed it from his mere presence?'

'Yes. And from the fact he ran away.'

'Quite so. You've told the court how you dropped to the
floor when the shot was fired and that Mr Wadingham did
likewise?'

'Yes.'

'In these circumstances, wouldn't it have been strange
if the defendant had continued standing at the counter?'

'I suppose it would.'

'So it's not really surprising that he made a quick departure?'

'Put like that, I suppose not.'

'Thank you, Miss Cunliffe,' Maxted said and, wrapping
his gown around him, sat down.

'This seems a suitable moment to break,' the judge
remarked, glancing at the wall clock. 'We'll resume at two
o'clock.' He turned towards the jury. 'Members of the jury,
let me remind you that you are trying this case according
to the evidence you hear in this court. Don't let anybody

tside speak to you about the case and don't discuss it with
ur families and friends when you go home this evening.
bove all, don't be influenced by anything you read about
in the press.'

His homily delivered, Judge Grapham strode off the bench
for lunch in the sheriff's dining-room.

Rosa and Paul Maxted crossed the street to the pub opposite and fought their way to the bar, where they were
eventually served with two glasses of white wine and a plate
of sandwiches.

Rosa knew that he would normally have had lunch in
the Bar mess and appreciated his gesture in accompanying
her to the pub.

'Difficult to know what's going through old Grapham's
head,' he remarked as he bit into a roast beef sandwich.
'He's kept unusually quiet for him. Perhaps that's a good
sign. I reckon the prosecution should complete its evidence
today. If so, we might just finish on Monday, though Tuesday
seems more likely.'

On their return to court, Rosa decided to go and have a
word with their client before the trial resumed. She found
him looking glum and depressed, a barely touched plate of
food in front of him.

'How are you feeling?' she asked, without hope of a
cheerful answer.

'It's not going well, is it?' he said in a grim tone.

'As well as Mr Maxted and I expected,' she replied stoutly.

'I'd hoped Mr Maxted would really tear Uncle Bernard
apart. As well as his bitch of a wife.'

'Cross-examination doesn't mean leaving the witness
bleeding on the floor. In fact, Mr Maxted cross-examined
both of them subtly and effectively. Your uncle was shown
as being prejudiced on the basis of false assumptions. The
same went for Mrs Hammond.'

'I just hope you're right.'

'As you know, the vital stage is yet to come. Namely,
when you give evidence.'

'When'll that be?'

'Monday.' She glanced at her watch. 'I've promised to call your wife this evening. She'll want to know how things have gone, also when she'll be required to give evidence.'

'I wish she didn't need to.'

'You want all the help you can get. Anyway, I'm sure she'll be an impressive witness in the sense of appearing decent and honest, and that can't do you any harm with the jury.'

She got up to leave when he said, 'What's happened to Superintendent Forrester? I've only seen Cleave in court.'

'He's in hospital and won't be giving evidence.'

'Serve him right!' He stared past Rosa, a distant expression on his face. 'Do you know I had to keep on pinching myself this morning to realise it was me they were talking about all the time? Me who's bloody innocent, sitting there in a cooking pot and being boiled for the feast.'

Rosa returned to court in a sombre mood. More than ever she prayed that justice, as she saw it, didn't take the wrong turn.

The afternoon was taken up with the evidence of Philip Wadingham, the eighteen-stone Alistair Yates and Detective Inspector Cleave. There were a couple of other police officers who filled in the story with items of uncontroverted testimony.

Wadingham seemed to have re-established his heroism in his own eyes and gave the impression that much worse things would have happened had he not been there to prevent them.

He agreed with defending counsel that the telephone call he took earlier in the morning was almost certainly from the defendant, though he hadn't immediately recognised his voice. He also agreed that if Lumley wished to visit his uncle, it was reasonable to phone in advance to find out that he would be in. Moreover, he retracted what he had said earlier about the caller trying to disguise his voice.

'He just sounded a bit hoarse,' he said in answer to Maxted.

'As if he had a cold?'

'Yes, it could have been that.'

Counsel had gone on, 'Were you aware that the defendant hadn't seen Mr Hammond for several months following a row between them?'

'Yes, Mrs Hammond had told me something to that effect. Not that it was any of my business,' he added quickly in an ingratiating tone.

'Looking back on events now, do you not think that the defendant's expression when he entered the shop was consistent with that of a nervous nephew hoping to make things up with his uncle?'

'Yes, I suppose it could have been,' said the witness, who plainly wished to be on everyone's side.

'So that when you said he looked furtive, you don't imply anything sinister by the use of that word?'

'I think I said he looked nervous . . . '

'Your exact words were, "nervous, even furtive".'

'Oh, I see what you mean. No, I just meant that he looked anxious and worried.'

'Thank you, Mr Wadingham, that's all I want to ask you.'

Counsel was about to sit down when Rosa leaned forward, gave his gown a small tug and whispered something in his ear.

Maxted nodded, murmured 'thank you' and straightened up again.

'There is a further matter I should have put to you,' he said. 'In answer to Mr Hobden, you testified that just before the shot was fired, the man with the revolver spoke to Lumley. Is that right?'

'Yes, but I never heard what he said.'

'Don't anticipate me, Mr Wadingham. You then added that you had the impression they weren't strangers to one another.'

'Yes.'

'What gave you that impression?'

'It was just an impression.'

'It must have been based on something?'

'It was the way the man looked at Mr Lumley.'

'Describe it.'

The witness squirmed. 'I can't. It was just a look.'

'Did he turn towards the defendant as he spoke to him?'

'Yes.'

'Which meant that he turned away from you?'

'Yes, sort of.'

'Either he did or he didn't, which was it?'

'He turned away.'

'And yet you were still able to observe the look on his face?'

'It was only a fleeting impression.'

'A *fleeting* impression, eh?'

'Yes,' the witness said uncomfortably.

'Do you think it may have been an impression conjured up after the event by your imagination?'

'I can't be too sure. Everything was happening at once, you see.'

'And the gun going off must have given you a nasty shock.'

'It certainly did.'

'A terrifying experience?'

'Yes.'

'Enough to blur the memory of the precise details of what happened?'

'I'm doing my best.'

'I'm sure you are,' counsel said with a friendly smile and this time sat down.

Alistair Yates, who followed him into the witness-box, gave the appearance of an outsize Jack popping out of a too-small box, as he stood taking the oath.

There was only one issue on which Maxted felt he needed to cross-examine and that was the suggestion that Lumley had dithered on the pavement outside the shop before running away.

'When you say dither, Mr Yates, do you mean anything more than that he hesitated a second before running off and meeting his nemesis in you?'

The witness was thoughtful for a moment.

'No, I don't suppose I do mean anything more than that,' he said genially. 'As a matter of fact, I don't think the word "dither" was mine. It came from the officer who was writing my statement.'

'As far as you were concerned, the defendant was merely somebody running along a pavement from what appeared to be the scene of a crime?'

'That about describes it, yes.'

'And being a public-spirited citizen, you decided to intervene?'

'Yes.'

'Was there considerable confusion in the street at the time?'

'There was a good deal of shouting and people running and this car accelerating away like a bat out of hell, if you'll excuse a non-legal expression.' He glanced toward the judge who didn't however look up from his notebook.

'By which time you were sitting on top of the defendant on the pavement?'

'Yes.'

'He offered no resistance?'

'Our relative sizes ensured that,' Yates replied with a grin. This time the judge allowed himself a small, steely smile.

The last witness of the day was Detective Inspector Cleave, who, more than ever, resembled a successful city executive in his well-pressed dark suit and purple and white striped shirt. He might have been the recently promoted head of department in a merchant bank. He gave his evidence clearly and dispassionately and faced Paul Maxted confidently when he rose to cross-examine.

'By the time you arrived on the scene, Mr Cleave, everything was over?' Maxted began.

'Yes, sir.'

'All you had to do was cart the defendant off to the station and interrogate him?'

'I take it you don't mean that literally, sir?' After a pause he went on, 'When I arrived in Firley Street, the defendant had already been taken away. My first task was to interview all the eye-witnesses I could find. It was one and a half to two hours before I returned to the station and saw the defendant.'

'Would I be right in thinking that you approached him sure

in your own mind that he had taken part in the robbery?'

'Yes.'

'Because that is what you were told by the people you'd interviewed at the scene?'

'That was certainly the sum of their information.'

'Was the defendant perfectly willing to be interviewed?'

Cleave pursed his lips. 'Yes, you could say that.'

'And in due course he made a written statement under caution?'

'He did.'

'And from beginning to end did he resolutely deny having participated in the robbery?'

'Yes.'

'Have you tried to test the truth of what he told you?'

The witness frowned. 'Test in what way, sir?'

'To find out if he mightn't be as innocent as he proclaimed?'

'If I may say so, sir, his denials didn't carry great conviction in the light of the evidence against him.'

'Is that still your view?'

'It's not for me to say, sir. It's a matter for the jury.'

'What steps have you taken to trace the men who got away?'

Cleave sighed. 'We've made extensive enquiries, sir, but I regret to say, have had no success at all. Their identities remain a total mystery.'

'No sign of the stolen property turning up anywhere?'

'None.'

'What about the getaway car?'

'That was discovered half a mile away from Firley Street. It failed to offer up any clues. There were no identifiable fingerprints other than those of its owner from outside whose house it had been stolen a week earlier. It had been fitted with false plates.'

'I believe the insurance company has offered a substantial reward for information leading to the arrest and conviction of the two missing men?'

'That's quite correct.'

'But even that hasn't raised a ripple?'

'Nothing that's reached our ears, sir.'

'Does that surprise you?'

Cleave fingered his chin thoughtfully before replying.

'It means one of two things in my opinion. Either those who could tell us something are too frightened to do so. Or it was a tightly-knit operation with only the participants in the know.'

'Has nobody been able to give a description of the driver of the getaway car?'

'Unfortunately not. Presumably he did nothing to draw attention to himself.'

'Except be double-parked?'

'I'm afraid that's not a particularly noteworthy occurrence in London these days,' Cleave replied in a wry tone.

'Is it right that the defendant has totally denied knowing the identities of the men who got away?'

'Yes.' The monosyllable was invested with enough scepticism to give it fresh meaning.

It was plain to Maxted that he would get no further change out of the witness and that it would be best to sit down. Experienced police officers are not given to collapsing under cross-examination and counsel felt he had achieved as much as he could.

Cleave was about to leave the witness-box when the judge addressed him.

'In your experience, officer, do innocent people often become incriminated in armed robberies?'

'I have never known it, my lord.'

Giving the jury a meaningful look, Judge Grapham announced that the court would stand adjourned to Monday.

'That was a monstrous question,' Rosa said indignantly to Paul Maxted.

'Sometimes they just can't resist putting the boot in. At least we now know where we stand.' He gave Rosa a tired smile. 'Good luck over the weekend. I'll get here early on Monday morning and you can then put me in the picture about Fingle.' He glanced at his watch. 'Perhaps we ought to go down to the cells to try and cheer our chap up.'

Chapter 10

Ben had managed to trace Fingle through a German girl named Renate, with whom he, Fingle, had shared a flat in Battersea. In fact there had been six of them (four English boys and two foreign girls) sharing the top two floors of a down-at-heel house, whose owner's only interest was the rent he could extort.

Renate was apparently in love with Les Fingle and had been upset when he moved down to Brighton. She kept in touch with him, however, and sought to make an ally out of Ben, something which suited both of them.

Early in the new year, Fingle left Brighton and for a while was once more adrift, though Renate was confident he would re-surface in her life.

'He needs me,' she kept saying to Ben. 'He will come back.'

And sure enough he did, though not till the middle of March when he returned to Battersea and to Renate's warm and comforting embrace.

Ben had managed to persuade the German girl that his own interest in Fingle was entirely benign. He spun her a story to the effect that Fingle was the only person who could help him trace a long lost relative. Being a girl with a singularly incurious mind, she accepted what he told her.

At all events, it was a Friday evening soon after Fingle's reappearance that he and Ben met at a pub. Rosa, who had been kept apprised of events, agreed that Ben should handle this initial meeting on his own. If it was fruitful, she would attend a subsequent meeting and make her own judgment of Fingle's usefulness as a potential witness. At that stage

71

she had small hope of anything productive emerging from contact with Bernard Hammond's ex-employee.

'What'll it be, mate?' Ben enquired, flashing a wallet stuffed with notes from Snaith and Epton's petty cash account. Fingle noted the money as he was intended to.

'A Scotch. Better make it a double.'

'Sure. Anything with it?'

Fingle shook his head as though the question was superfluous.

Armed with their drinks (Ben's was a pint of bitter) they retired to a corner of the saloon bar and sat down.

'Cheers, mate,' Ben said, raising his glass.

'Cheers,' Fingle murmured.

Ben reckoned it had been some time since anyone had stood him a large Scotch and he seemed intent on enjoying it. Moreover, the sight of Ben's wallet held out promise of another.

'What is it you're after?' he asked, putting his glass down on the table and fixing Ben with a hard look.

Ben grinned. He specialised in disarming grins when cornered.

'I believe you once worked for Bernard Hammond, the jewellers?' he said.

Fingle's look sharpened. 'What's it to you where I've worked?' His tone was wary and carried a note of hostility.

Ben took a deep breath. 'I work in a solicitor's office and we have a client who's had a spot of bother with Hammond's.'

'So?'

'If you once worked there, you might be able to help.'

Fingle picked up his glass and half-drained it. Then he gave a shrug.

'You obviously know I did once work there. So what?'

'How'd you get on with old Hammond himself?'

Fingle finished off his drink and pushed the glass into the middle of the table.

'What about a refill?' he said.

'Good idea,' Ben said, springing up and heading for the bar. When he returned, Fingle had lit a cigarette and was observing its burning tip with frowning concentration.

'You were about to tell me how you got on with old Hammond,' Ben remarked.

'I got the sack, which you presumably know. He accused me of dishonesty and dismissed me without so much as a week's notice.'

'He sounds a right old bastard.'

'What sort of trouble is your client in?'

'Did you read about an armed robbery at Hammond's shop last October?'

Though Fingle's expression never changed, Ben felt a sudden tension in the air.

'What about it?'

'The thieves got away with over £100,000 worth of stuff and old Hammond got a bullet through his shoulder.'

'I seem to remember reading something about it,' Fingle said in an off-hand tone.

'The robbers got away,' Ben went on, 'they've never been caught.'

'You won't find them hiding under my bed. I'd say good luck to them.'

'Hammond's nephew, Stephen Lumley, happened to be in the shop at the time and was arrested, even though he's completely innocent.'

'Tough luck.'

'You'd think it was more than that if you were in his place.'

Fingle shrugged. 'Why are you telling me all this?'

'We're trying to trace people who used to work at Hammond's to see if any of them may be able to help.'

'Help in what way?'

'Throw light on the background . . . '

'There doesn't have to be a background.' His tone was aggressively emphatic. But then somewhat lamely he added, 'What makes you think there is?'

'Because it's the sort of crime that does have a background,'

Ben said. 'We get to recognise them in our line of business. By the way what do you think of Carol Hammond?'

'She was Carol Upshaw when I was there.'

He's obviously kept in touch, thought Ben, or he wouldn't know she had married the boss.

'Ambitious lady from all I hear,' he said.

Fingle gave him a long, thoughtful look, then picking up his glass, he tossed back his drink and said, 'I've got to be going. Thanks for the Scotch.'

Leaving his own drink unfinished, Ben quickly rose. 'I'd like you to meet one of the partners in my firm,' he said with a note of urgency.

'What for?'

'It could help an innocent man.'

'If you believe I'm a knight in shining armour, forget it. My own skin is more important to me than anyone else's.'

'But your own skin wouldn't be involved.'

'That's what you think.'

Before Ben could make any reply, Fingle had shot out of the pub. By the time Ben reached the door he had vanished.

'I'm dead certain he knows something, Miss E,' Ben said to Rosa the next day.

Rosa was duly impressed by what Ben reported to her, though whether Fingle could really help Lumley's defence had yet to be determined.

There followed, however, weeks of frustration with Fingle seemingly having disappeared for good. Renate claimed to have no knowledge of his whereabouts and was inclined to blame Ben for his vanishing act. She clearly felt he had deceived her and didn't deserve her further co-operation.

'You lie to me,' she said accusingly when he called at the address in Battersea. 'You frighten Les and he does not wish to see you again. Nor do I.'

Nothing Ben could say would change her mind.

Then just two days before Lumley's trial opened, Ben received a postcard at the office. It read:

Be at Queen Adelaide pub, London Road, Reading
at six on Saturday.
    LF

It was this appointment that absorbed Rosa's thoughts
as she left the Old Bailey that Friday afternoon.

Rosa met Ben outside Shepherd's Bush underground station
at four thirty the next afternoon and they set off for Reading
in Rosa's small Honda. It was an oppressively hot afternoon
with a total absence of sunshine. The sky was leaden with
ominous tinges of yellow.

Ben was as excited as a small boy being given a special
treat and wriggled about in his seat.

'Just hope it's not a hoax,' he said as they went a steady
sixty m.p.h. down the M4.

'Whatever else it's unlikely to be that,' Rosa observed.
'Whether or not he turns up is a different matter. And even
if he does, it still doesn't mean we'll learn anything to our
advantage.'

'Can't see why he bothered to get in touch unless he's ready
to talk,' Ben said, rubbing his hands together in anticipation
of what lay ahead.

'I agree,' Rosa said, 'but he may be having second thoughts.
He doesn't sound the most reliable of people.'

'Do you remember the first time we met, Miss E?' he
asked suddenly.

'It was at Ealing Magistrates' Court.'

'That's right. I was up on a housebreaking charge. I'd
thought the occupants had gone away, but they suddenly
walked in and caught me having a nosh-up in their kitchen.'

'With some of their family silver in a Harrods carrier
bag beside you, if I rightly remember.'

Ben laughed. 'I thought the Harrods bag was a nice touch.
I was rather pleased with that.'

'I don't think you'd ever have been a very successful
burglar, Ben.'

'I reckon I'd have improved. I learnt quite a bit while
I was in detention. Nevertheless, I'm glad I came asking

you for a job instead. I never really expected you to give me one.'

'It was touch and go.'

Ben let out a sigh. 'I guess life's made up of knife-edge decisions. One'll never know how different things might have been if one had decided to turn left instead of right.'

'Stop philosophising and tell me how to get to the Queen Adelaide pub,' Rosa said, as they left the motorway on the outskirts of Reading.

A bit further on she stopped the car and Ben enquired the way of an old man sitting on a seat at a bus-stop.

The Queen Adelaide was a newish public house on the outskirts of the town. It was set back from the road and had a paved forecourt on which there were tables and chairs to give it a beer-garden appearance. Striped umbrellas advertised the brewery's products. There was a park on the opposite side of the road with tennis courts and a children's playground.

'He's not here yet,' Ben said, glancing around the bar. 'Let me buy you a drink, Miss E.'

'This is a business outing, so drinks are on Snaith and Epton,' Rosa said. 'I'll have a Campari and orange juice with ice.' She opened her bag and passed Ben a £5 note.

''Fraid that won't go far, if he's still on double Scotches,' Ben observed.

'He may never come,' Rosa replied, firmly closing her bag.

'Decided I'd have the same,' Ben said as he rejoined her from the bar with their drinks. 'Cheers.'

Ten minutes later, Rosa said, 'He's not going to turn up. He's taken fright; or more likely, never intended coming.'

'Not everyone's as punctual as you are, Miss E. There's still lots of time for him to appear.'

'Meanwhile, you and I drink away the firm's profits.'

'Hold it, he's just come in,' Ben exclaimed a moment later.

Rosa looked toward the door and saw a thin-faced young man. He had straight dark hair, a lick of which fell across his forehead like a car windscreen wiper. Before he had spotted them, Ben had jumped up and gone over to him. Rosa observed the young man stare suspiciously in her direction. Then with a sullen expression he followed Ben to where she was sitting.

'This is Les Fingle,' Ben announced. 'I'll just fetch him a drink.'

'I'm glad you've come,' Rosa said, feeling unusually inhibited. 'You could be the break we're looking for. Ben's told you about the case, I believe.'

Fingle said nothing. Indeed, he appeared to be undecided whether to stay. Fortunately at that moment Ben arrived back at the table, bearing a large Scotch.

Fingle took the glass from him and immediately drank half of the contents. He was clearly tense and nervous and Rosa noticed that his hand shook as he put down the glass.

'I'm just going to the toilet,' he mumbled, getting to his feet.

'Me, too,' Ben said quickly as he rose to follow him.

Rosa half-expected Ben to return alone and announce that Fingle had given him the slip. She was, therefore, relieved when they rejoined her at the table.

'I've been telling Les about the trial,' Ben remarked, 'and how our client can do with all the help he can get.'

Rosa nodded keenly. 'Can you suggest a possible line of enquiry, Les?'

Fingle stared into his now empty glass, but said nothing.

Rosa went on, 'The trial will end on Tuesday, so we are up against time. Is there anything you can tell us about Bernard Hammond that might throw a different light on everything?'

Fingle gave her a strange look.

'Is Lumley likely to get off?' he asked abruptly.

Rosa gave a helpless shrug. 'I'm certain he's innocent, but the judge is against him and I don't fancy his chances. That's why Ben and I have kept this rendezvous. You wouldn't have sent Ben that card unless you had something important to say. Please tell us what it is.'

Fingle shook his head in a perplexed manner.

'I shouldn't have sent the card,' he muttered.

'You didn't think that at the time,' Rosa said.

'Have another Scotch,' Ben said, springing up and seizing his empty glass.

'If Lumley gets off, everything'll be all right,' Fingle remarked while Ben was fighting his way to the bar.

'But what if he doesn't?' Rosa said in a tone of great urgency. 'It's shattering to think of an innocent man spending the coming years of his life behind bars.'

'I've got to have more time to think,' Fingle said with a sudden note of desperation.

'There isn't any time left.'

Then before Rosa could say anything further, Les Fingle had leapt to his feet and fled from the bar.

When Ben returned with the drinks, he found Rosa sitting alone. She told him what had happened.

'The rat,' Ben observed equably. 'What are we going to do now, Miss E?'

'Go home. Our only hope is that he'll get in touch again.'

'He's sure to see the result of the case in the paper.'

'Provided he looks out for it.'

Ben was silent for a while, then he said, 'I wonder what it is he knows.'

'And, if we ever find out, what good it'll do Stephen Lumley.'

Chapter 11

Rosa decided that she must call Paul Maxted at home on Sunday and let him know what had happened.

His wife, whom she had never met, answered the phone, though Rosa knew her voice from previous phone calls to their house.

'I do apologise for disturbing him on a Sunday,' she said.

'He's mowing the lawn and will welcome the interruption,' Claudine Maxted replied drily. 'Hold on a moment and I'll give him a shout.'

A couple of minutes later he came on the line.

''Morning, Rosa. You couldn't have timed your call better. Now I'll be able to bribe one of the children to finish the lawn for me. They're a mercenary lot. How was your visit to Reading?'

'As you've probably guessed, that's why I'm phoning you,' Rosa said and went on to tell him of its unsatisfactory outcome. She concluded, 'It's plain that he knows something, but who's to tell whether or not it could help our case. That's what makes it so frustrating. If one could write him off as a waste of time, it would be that much simpler, but one can't.'

'I find it hard to think of any evidence he could give which would enhance our client's chances of acquittal,' Maxted said in a reflective tone. 'I'm not saying he mayn't know something to Hammond's discredit, but that doesn't of itself assist our case. I don't really see what more we can do.' Before Rosa could say anything he went on, 'We can't possibly ask for an adjournment on the flimsy ground that there may be a witness

79

who could help the defence, but we don't know where he is or exactly what his evidence would be. We couldn't even have sought a postponement of the trial before it began on such insubstantial grounds.'

Rosa hadn't really expected Paul Maxted to react in any other way. He was a practical and experienced counsel and the ultimate responsibility for the conduct of the case was his. Moreover she knew he didn't share her conviction of Lumley's innocence.

'Do you agree?' he now said.

'I think what you've said is unarguable, Paul. I suppose I hoped you might come up with some inspired suggestion.'

'Inspiration isn't my forte, I'm afraid,' he remarked with a laugh.

'What do you think I should try and do to trace Fingle?'

'Ben seems to have done pretty well to date. I suppose he could case some of Fingle's more likely haunts in Reading, though I'd feel personally inclined to wait until Fingle renews contact. From what you've told me there's a reasonable chance he'll do that if Lumley goes down. In which case he might provide us with ammunition for an appeal.'

'I wonder if Inspector Cleave might be disposed to help,' Rosa said thoughtfully.

'The police aren't going to assist unless you can give them something solid to go on. If Lumley's convicted, they'll close their file and certainly won't be interested in chasing some will o' the wisp.'

'How can they close their file with two robbers still at large? Whatever the outcome of Lumley's trial, they can't fool themselves they've solved the case.'

Maxted let out a quiet sigh. 'It's my guess that they'll sit back and wait for clues to come to them. They won't be taking any initiatives on their own.' He paused. 'I know it goes against the grain, Rosa, but I really don't see there's anything further we can do at this stage. Once the trial is over, we'll be better able to review the whole situation.'

'OK, I'll now let you get back to the lawn,' Rosa said.

'If the lawn sees me again this morning, it'll be with a

large gin and tonic in my hand. Anyway, thanks for calling, Rosa. Till tomorrow at the Bailey.'

As she made her way to the court cells the next morning, Rosa was glad that she hadn't told Lumley of her intended visit to Reading. It would inevitably have raised his hopes, which was the very reason she had not informed him. If it turned out to be a fruitful visit, there would be time enough to tell him. As things were, however, this was the last moment to dash his expectations. With the prospect of giving evidence that day, he was certain to be in a state of high nervous tension.

'How are you feeling this morning?' Rosa enquired in a brisk bedside manner.

'Terrible.'

'Once you're in the witness-box and have got used to hearing your own voice in court, you'll be all right. Remember, all you have to do is tell the truth. If you stick to the truth, no amount of cross-examination can confuse you.'

It was rare that she felt able to give this particular piece of advice to a client. For most, the truth was something to be glossed over, skated round and generally fenced with. From his expression, however, Lumley was far from reassured.

'Is there anything you want to ask me before the court sits?' Rosa asked. He shook his head in a morose fashion. 'Did you see Christine over the weekend?' He gave a nod and Rosa went on, 'Not every defendant has a wife who supports him all the way. I think the jury will take to her.'

'She still won't be able to save me.'

'That's defeatist talk. Try and think of all the people rooting for you, but remember that the major effort has to come from you. This is your D-Day, so be determined not to let yourself down.'

Rosa could see, however, that her words were largely wasted. It was unfortunate that he had had the weekend to brood in a prison cell. It was the worst possible preparation for his coming ordeal. And ordeal it would certainly prove to be; almost as much for Rosa as for him.

Fifteen minutes later the judge took his seat and the tableau being enacted in court eight was once more in place.

'I call the defendant,' Paul Maxted said.

Rosa watched Stephen Lumley make his way from dock to witness-box, followed by a prison officer who would sit nearby and be a reminder that this was 'the prisoner at the bar' who was giving evidence.

'Is your name Stephen Lumley and are you twenty-nine years old?' counsel asked briskly.

The witness nodded.

'I'm afraid the shorthand-writer can't record nods, so perhaps you'd answer the question.'

'As I heard it, Mr Maxted, there were two questions,' the judge remarked.

'That's so, my lord. I was attempting not to waste the court's time on undisputed issues.'

'In my experience, Mr Maxted, more time is wasted in court when counsel try and take short-cuts, than in any other way.'

'If your lordship pleases.' Paul Maxted turned once more towards the witness who, not without justification, was wearing a somewhat bewildered expression. 'Let me begin again. Is your name Stephen Lumley?'

'Yes.'

'And are you twenty-nine years old?'

'Yes.'

'Married?'

'Yes.'

'Do you have any children?'

'Two.'

'What are their ages?'

'The boy's six and the girl is three.'

'Is yours a happy marriage?'

'Yes. At least it was until all this happened.'

Counsel went on to elicit details of the defendant's employment in the months preceding the robbery.

'Had Mr Hammond, your uncle, usually been ready to assist you financially when you were in difficulty?'

'Yes, he'd been very generous to me.'

'So what was your reaction when you visited him at his home one evening last July and were refused further help?'

'I was extremely upset.'

'And?'

'I'm afraid I lost my cool and let my tongue run away with me.'

'What exactly did you say?'

'I told him he'd live to regret his refusal to lend me money.'

'Did you at that time have it in mind to seek some form of physical revenge?'

'Definitely not. I just felt upset at the way things had turned out.' He hesitated a second, then blurted out, 'I was pretty sure that my uncle's new wife had turned him against me.'

Pity he said that, Rosa reflected. She glanced quickly at the jury to catch their reaction, but learnt nothing. They had their heads turned towards the witness-box and were observing Lumley with attentive expressions.

It seemed clear that counsel shared Rosa's view of the observation for he now quickly went on, 'Let us now come to Wednesday, 28th October last year. Did you reach a certain decision that morning?'

Lumley passed his tongue across his lips. 'Yes. I'd been wanting to make things up with Uncle Bernard, I mean Mr Hammond, for some time and I decided to go and see him. I was going to apologise for having lost my temper with him when I visited him in July.'

'Any reason for choosing that particular day?'

'The next day was my daughter's birthday and my uncle was very fond of both my children. You see, he'd never had any of his own and he used to treat mine like grand-children.'

'So what did you do before you set out that morning?'

'I phoned the shop to make sure he was there.'

'To whom did you speak?'

'Philip Wadingham.'

'Did you attempt to disguise your voice?'

'Definitely not. If it sounded different, it was because I was feeling nervous.'

A few questions later, Maxted asked, 'Did you tell your wife where you were going?'

'Yes.'

'How did you travel to Firley Street?'

'By bus.'

'And as you approached the shop, did everything appear normal?'

'Yes.'

'What happened next?'

'I went in and approached Miss Cunliffe at the counter. I said I'd come to see my uncle. I'd hardly spoken before these two men came in and stood alongside me. One had a gun which he pointed at Mr Wadingham while the other began smashing the showcase with a hammer.'

'What did you do?'

'I just couldn't believe what was happening. My uncle appeared in the doorway to the office and the man nearest to me fired the gun. Then they both dashed out.'

'What did you do?'

The question seemed to hang in the air while all eyes were focused expectantly on the witness. Lumley, for his part, looked around as though to keep everyone in suspense for as long as possible.

'I followed them,' he said in little more than a whisper.

'Followed them? Can you amplify that?'

'I dashed out too. I was in a blind panic. I just wanted to get away. I was totally shattered by what had happened. I knew it had happened and yet I couldn't take it in.'

'Which way did you run?'

'I ran along the pavement to my right, but then somebody tripped me and I fell.' He gave a helpless shrug which said, 'You know the rest'.

'Had you ever seen either of the two robbers before?'

'Never.'

'Have you any idea who they were?'

'Definitely not.'

'Have you benefited in any way from the robbery?'

'Benefited?' he echoed in a bitter voice. 'It's the most disastrous thing that's ever happened to me.' He put a hand up to his face to flick away a tear that was rolling down his cheek.

Rosa noticed that one of the motherly-looking jurors also appeared moist-eyed.

The core of Lumley's evidence was over and a few minutes later Maxted sat down. Rosa braced herself as prosecuting counsel rose to cross-examine. Seldom had she felt so involved in a client's fortunes.

For a few seconds, Oliver Hobden gazed at Lumley as though deliberating which side of an apple to take a first bite from.

'Would it be fair to say that at the time of the robbery you were flat broke?' he enquired politely.

'Yes. I had been for some time.'

'Flat broke and heavily in debt?'

'Yes.'

'Desperate for money?'

'Not so desperate as to rob my own uncle,' Lumley said angrily.

'Your major source of money had dried up, had it not?'

'If you mean my uncle, I resent that. My major source had always been my work.'

'But you'd been out of work for several months.'

'Yes.'

'Leaving your uncle as the only person to whom you felt you could turn?'

'Not the only person.'

'Who else?'

'There are always money-lenders.'

'Who charge exorbitant rates of interest. Did Mr Hammond ever charge interest on the money he lent you?'

'No.'

'But as you've told the court, you'd quarrelled with your uncle and he'd told you to stay out of his sight. That's right, isn't it?'

'Yes.'

'When exactly did you decide to rob him?'

'I was never part of the robbery,' Lumley said wearily.

'It was a highly profitable robbery, wasn't it?'

'So I gather.'

'I presume you knew that he kept a lot of valuable jewellery on the premises?'

'I'd never thought about it.'

'Is that what you're asking the jury to believe?'

'It's the truth.'

For several minutes prosecuting counsel continued to probe this angle of the case, suggesting that even if the defendant hadn't himself organised the robbery, he had been a very willing participant. Rosa felt that he was acquitting himself as well as she could have hoped. He was following her advice about answering questions shortly and not being drawn into saying more than was strictly necessary. So often she had seen witnesses, especially defendants, flounder through disregarding this tenet. The adage about giving a man enough rope and he'd hang himself was particularly relevant in a court of law.

'You must have been very shocked when you saw your uncle collapse, shot and bleeding?'

'Yes.'

'Did it not occur to you to go to his assistance?'

'I've tried to explain. I panicked.'

'Surely, if what you're telling the jury is true, it would have been the most natural thing to do, wouldn't it?'

'Everything happened so quickly,' Lumley murmured unhappily.

But prosecuting counsel knew he had a good point and wasn't ready to give up.

'I mean, you'd gone there with rapprochement as your aim, and here surely was a heaven-sent opportunity to show your intention by leaping to your injured uncle's assistance?'

'I've told you I panicked.'

'I know you have,' Hobden observed patiently, 'but I'm sure the jury would like to know why.'

It was apparent that Hobden felt he had torn a large enough hole in the defence case, for after a few further questions he sat down.

Lumley was about to leave the witness-box when Judge Grapham spoke.

'You say you went to your uncle's shop that day in order to effect a reconciliation?'

'Yes.'

'Why to his shop? Surely his home would have been a far better place for such a purpose?'

'He'd most likely have slammed the door in my face. He couldn't do that at the shop.'

It seemed to Rosa to be a good answer and her feeling was confirmed when the judge turned away with an imperious sniff. She had the impression that the jury was still uncommitted, even if the judge was not.

'I now call Mrs Lumley,' Paul Maxted said, after indicating that he didn't wish to re-examine.

Watching her take the oath, Rosa decided that she struck just the right note of nervousness and vulnerability to appeal to the jury. She was wearing a simple blue and white dress and scarcely any make-up.

After the usual opening questions, Maxted asked, 'What was your husband's reaction to the row he had last July with his uncle?'

'He was very upset about it. He said several times that he'd like to make things up with him. Uncle Bernard was his only surviving relative and Stephen had always liked him. He had been especially kind after Stephen's mother and father were killed.'

'And went on being kind and generous until that day in July?'

Christine Lumley bit her lip. 'Stephen hadn't been so much in touch with Uncle Bernard after he re-married.'

'Coming now to Wednesday, 28th October last, what time did the defendant go out that morning?'

'Just before eleven o'clock.'

'Did he tell you where he was going?'

87

'Yes, he'd made up his mind to go and see Mr Hammond at his shop to try and patch things up.'

'Is that what he told you?'

'Yes. He'd phoned earlier to make sure he'd be there.'

'Did you hear him make the call?'

The witness blushed. 'Our phone had been disconnected, so he had to use a call-box.'

'And when he left home just before eleven, was that the last you saw of him until after the robbery?'

'It was the last I saw of him until the next day. The first I knew anything about a robbery was around three o'clock when police burst into the flat. They told me Stephen had been arrested for taking part in a robbery.'

'What was your reaction?'

'I didn't believe them. I thought there was some terrible mistake.'

'Had the defendant ever said or done anything to make you think he was planning to rob his uncle?'

'Never.'

'Do you think you'd have known if he had been up to some such thing?'

She threw counsel a challenging look as she answered. 'Of course I'd have known. I always knew when he was keeping something from me.'

'Thank you, Mrs Lumley,' Maxted said and sat down.

'You sound very positive about that?' Hobden remarked as he rose and faced her across the court.

'I'm afraid I don't understand the question,' she said with a frown.

'Because it wasn't a question,' Paul Maxted observed just loud enough to be heard by those nearest to him.

Hobden ignored him. 'Did your husband always tell you everything he was going to do?' he asked.

'All the important things.'

'Would you agree that surprise is a vital ingredient in the commission of a robbery?'

'I've not thought about it.'

'Give it a bit of thought now and then answer my question.'

'Yes, I suppose it is,' she replied with a slight shrug.

'Those who are planning a robbery are unlikely to let everyone know what they are up to. Not even their wives. Would you agree?'

'If Stephen had been about to get involved in something like a robbery, I'd have known.'

'How?'

'How? Because I'm his wife and I know him inside out.'

'Are you saying he's never successfully deceived you?'

'How would she know if the deceit was successful?' Paul Maxted broke in.

'Let me put it this way, Mrs Lumley,' Hobden said with a mock bow to defending counsel. 'Has the defendant ever tried to deceive you and failed?'

'Not often.'

'You mean, there have been occasions when you caught him out?'

'A few.'

'May there not have been others when you didn't?'

Hobden didn't wait for an answer. It was the question that mattered and he didn't want a reply. He merely wished to give the jury the impression of a loyal wife whose evidence shouldn't be accepted at face value.

Rosa often felt that criminal courts were not unlike hospital operating theatres. As soon as one patient or defendant had been dealt with, a start was made on the next with the minimum of fuss. It might be the most vital day in the life of the person going under the legal or surgical knife, but to those in attendance, it was just another routine day. This impression was especially strong as a trial drew to its close and only speeches and a summing-up remained. It was doubtless different in bygone days when counsel were dramatic actors of the hammiest sort and the gallows or long terms of penal servitude awaited the hapless prisoner. But now everything had been toned down and advocacy was passion-free.

All this occurred to Rosa as she listened to Hobden making his final speech in a quiet, matter-of-fact voice.

'There's really very little dispute as to the facts of this case,' he observed toward the end of his speech. 'It's a matter of interpretation. The defence would like you to enter a world of fantasy and say that it was a pure coincidence the defendant happened to be in the shop at the very moment the robbery took place. The prosecution say that you mustn't ignore what your common sense must surely tell you, namely that Lumley participated in the robbery and must on the evidence be convicted.'

Judge Grapham glanced first at the clock and then at Paul Maxted.

'How long do you think you'll be, Mr Maxted?'

'About forty-five minutes, my lord.'

'That means you won't finish before the luncheon adjournment,' he said reproachfully. 'Well, you'd better begin. We can't waste a whole half hour of court time.'

He had been known to say that the best speeches, like the best sermons, were short ones. Certainly his directions to juries were usually models of conciseness, if not of impartiality. He was totally self-confident and never worried about what an appeal court might say.

Unperturbed by the judge's demeanour, Paul Maxted gave the jury a friendly, embracing look and began his final address.

'May it please your lordship, members of the jury, as my learned friend said to you a few minutes ago, the crux of this case rests upon your interpretation of the facts. He poured scorn on the possibility of the defendant's presence in the shop being a coincidence. But think for a moment of the coincidences that occur in all our daily lives: of the number of times we exclaim to each other, "What a coincidence!" Fortunately, members of the jury, most of them are unmemorable occurrences, but the fact is that they do occur. The coincidence that has landed the defendant in the dock of this court was a catastrophe which has threatened to destroy his life. Nevertheless, it was still a coincidence, no more and no less than the ones we soon forget. Let me review the evidence with you . . . '

Counsel had just completed this part of his address when the judge intervened.

'We'll adjourn now and resume at two o'clock.' He turned towards the jury. 'It should be possible to finish the case today,' he said, before stalking off the bench.

Paul Maxted asked Rosa to excuse him during the break. His clerk had brought over some papers from Chambers which he had to read in preparation for a conference at the end of the afternoon.

Rosa ate a quick sandwich and then went for a brisk walk in the environs of St Paul's where office workers and tourists were out in equal numbers. On her return to the Old Bailey she went to see Lumley. She didn't relish the visit, but felt it her duty to go.

'I don't bring news, either good or bad,' she said when he looked up at her entry.

'Do you think the jury believed me?' he asked.

'It's impossible to know what's going on in twelve different heads,' she replied with a helpless shrug.

'So you think I may be found guilty?' he said despairingly. 'Even though I'm innocent.'

'Even if you *are* convicted, there's always the appeal court.'

'But that could take months.'

'I know. All I can say is that I'll continue to fight for you for as long as it takes.'

'Don't think I'm not grateful for all you've done, Miss Epton, but I'd pinned my hopes on your being able to find out what really happened, as the police have obviously given up on the case.'

A few minutes later they were all back in court.

'Yes, Mr Maxted,' the judge said briskly as soon as he was seated. 'I don't think you'd quite finished when we adjourned.'

'No, my lord, I hadn't,' Maxted said, as though daring the judge to pass further comment.

Twenty minutes or so later, he reached his peroration.

'I ask you to say, members of the jury, that this was an outrageous coincidence which befell the defendant and to bear firmly in your minds that, apart from his physical presence in the shop, there isn't a whisper of evidence to connect him with the crime. His fate rests in your hands, members of the jury, and I ask you to find him not guilty.'

Judge Grapham glanced at the wall clock which showed the time as two twenty-eight, then held a whispered colloquy with the clerk of the court and finally turned to face the jury.

'Members of the jury, the facts of this case fall within a small compass, as both counsel have been at pains to tell you. And facts are entirely a matter for you. If I happen to express a view with which you disagree, then disregard it. You are the sole judges of fact, my rôle being to advise you as to the law and to assist you to reach a decision on the evidence.'

After these preliminary observations he went on to direct them as to the burden of proof in a criminal case. 'It is for the prosecution to satisfy you beyond reasonable doubt that the defendant is guilty. If they have failed to discharge that burden, then you should acquit.' He next defined the offences of robbery and wounding with intent, concluding, 'though in this case it is beyond dispute that a robbery took place and a gun was fired whereby Mr Hammond was wounded. The only point at issue is whether the defendant took part.' There followed a brisk review of the evidence. 'Members of the jury, if you really think that the defendant's presence was a coincidence – and as I've already said, the facts are for you, though you shouldn't leave your common sense behind in judging them – then I suggest you should ask yourselves why he ran away from the shop? Was it an act of panic, as he says, or was it an act more consistent with guilt? You may think that the prosecution's case is a compelling one, in which event it would be your duty to convict. The fact that others not before the court were involved is irrelevant to your consideration of the evidence against Lumley. Moreover, I would strongly advise you not to indulge in speculation in that particular realm. The case against the defendant is that he took part in the robbery as a principal in the first degree.

Moreover, if you conclude that the carrying of a loaded gun, with a view to using it if necessary, was part of the joint venture, then the defendant is as guilty as the person who actually fired it.'

It was precisely three o'clock when Judge Grapham concluded his summing-up and the twelve jurors trooped out of court in the wake of the jury bailiff. There was a ten-minute adjournment after which the judge was returning to court to deal with a number of applications in other cases.

'Why's he in such a rush?' Maxted said to the clerk of the court during the interval. 'Supposing the jury can't reach a decision in the time it takes to smoke a cigarette?'

The clerk gave a resigned shrug. 'He reckons they shouldn't need more than an hour to arrive at a verdict and he wants to get the whole thing disposed of this afternoon. He's not sitting tomorrow.'

'Where's he off to? Some golf course or other?'

'Oh, no, nothing as frivolous as that. He's attending a family funeral.'

Half an hour later Judge Grapham had dealt with the various applications and had retired to his room to await the jury's return to court. A further hour went by and the jury was still out. Meanwhile, all the other courts had risen for the day. Paul Maxted had phoned his Chambers to cancel the conference that his clerk had arranged.

At half past five the clerk returned to court and informed counsel that the judge was proposing to send for the jury and, if necessary, give them directions as to a majority verdict.

'He reckons there's probably one juror holding out,' the clerk said. 'As they've had the required minimum time to reach a verdict, he's proposing to force the issue.'

'Two and a half hours in a serious robbery case isn't all that long,' Maxted observed. 'I deplore such unseemly haste.'

The clerk gave him a helpless smile as the jury was shepherded back into court. Rosa anxiously scanned their faces.

Two of the motherly-looking women appeared flushed and the third (the coloured lady) gave the impression of having been involved in a family row. The woman with the built-in harassed air looked rather more harassed than before. On the other hand the smartly dressed female looked as though she had just won a board-room battle.

Of the men, the oriental youth remained his impassive self; the young man in black leather with streaked hair had a mutinous expression; and the five older men continued to look like the upright citizens they might even be.

In all, Rosa decided that they didn't present a reassuring spectacle. Even before they returned to the box, it had become clear there was a contest of wills going on in the jury-room.

The clerk stood up and addressed them.

'Have you reached a verdict on which you are all agreed? Please answer "yes" or "no".'

The foreman, who looked to be the oldest man on the jury, rose to his feet.

'No,' he said in a loud voice.

The judge now took over and explained he would accept a majority verdict if they were unable to reach unanimity, but that at least ten of them must agree on the verdict. He said they should still try and reach a unanimous verdict and reminded them of the oath they had taken. He also spoke of the public inconvenience and expense if jurors couldn't agree owing to the unwillingness of one or two of their number to listen to the arguments of the rest.

Once more they trooped out of court to return about half an hour later.

'Have at least ten of you agreed upon your verdict?' the clerk asked.

'Yes.'

'What is your verdict? Please only answer guilty or not guilty.'

'Guilty, by a majority of ten to two,' the foreman announced in a forthright tone. Turning toward the judge he went on, 'We should like to add a rider, my lord.'

The judge frowned. 'It's not usual: indeed— '

Before he could say more, however, the foreman boldly

went on, 'We should like to say we accept that the defendant played a lesser rôle than the others in the robbery. That's all, my lord, thank you.'

The judge's expression warned of his displeasure at the foreman's conduct. Rosa, meanwhile, glanced round at Lumley. He was staring straight ahead of him, his gaze fixed high on the opposite wall. She was thankful that his wife had taken her advice to stay out of court. The last thing a defendant needed was to have a weeping, less still hysterical, wife in court when he was about to be sentenced.

DI Cleave went into the witness-box and gave evidence of 'antecedents', while the judge began to show increasing signs of impatience.

Paul Maxted made a short but effective plea in mitigation which, all could see, was falling on deaf ears. He asked the judge to take into account the jury's rider.

He hardly had time to sit down before the judge began addressing the defendant.

'Stephen Lumley, the jury have found you guilty on the clearest possible evidence. You took part in a dastardly crime and now you must pay the penalty. You must go to prison for six years.'

Rosa and Paul Maxted were the last two people to leave the court in the now silent building. Somewhere below them Stephen Lumley waited to be taken away to prison to serve his sentence. The echoing sound of a distant cell door being shut came as a reminder, if one were needed.

'I know you're disappointed, Rosa, but it's a result that was always on the cards.'

'I'm not so much disappointed as seething with frustration. A monstrous injustice has been done.'

Maxted gave a weary shrug. 'Maybe you're right, maybe not. I hope not as nobody wants to think of an innocent person spending years in prison.'

'We must lodge an appeal, Paul. I'd like you to draft the grounds.'

'I take it you mean an appeal against sentence.'

'Conviction and sentence.'

'I'm not sure we have any grounds for an appeal against conviction. Grapham's summing-up mayn't have been as fair as one would have hoped, but it contained no misdirections in law, and one can't say that his majority verdict direction put the jury under untimely pressure. As to sentence, one might persuade the Court of Appeal to knock off a year, but even that is doubtful. If there'd been any evidence that Lumley himself was armed, he'd have got ten years.'

'His conviction was against the weight of the evidence,' Rosa said fiercely.

Maxted sighed. 'The Court of Appeal is always at pains to say that it won't usurp the functions of a jury. If the jury's verdict is reasonable on the evidence, they won't upset it; even though, as we all know, a different jury might have returned a different verdict. That's why it's all a bit of a lottery. Of course everything could change if the other two robbers are ever caught. That must be Lumley's main hope.'

Rosa said nothing. She didn't dissent from anything counsel had said, apart from his references to the *other* two robbers. His words had served to fuel her determination to dig deeper into the Firley Street jewel robbery.

If Stephen Lumley was innocent, then somebody must be well aware of the fact. Somebody whose interests had been served by his conviction: somebody for whom concealment of the truth was absolutely vital.

Chapter 12

'It was a grave miscarriage of justice,' Rosa said emphatically.

'I know that's your gut feeling, but you could be wrong,' Robin Snaith said patiently the next day when he and Rosa met in the office. 'Nobody can say it was a perverse verdict on the evidence. The jury chose to believe that Lumley was there as a robber and not an innocent spectator.'

'Anyway, what am I going to do, Robin?'

'Forget about it,' he said crisply.

Rosa stared at him in astonishment.

'How can I possibly do that?'

'You either do it or finish up a paranoiac.'

'You mean, you're content to accept meekly a miscarriage of justice?'

He sighed. 'We both know that they occur from time to time. It's inevitable in any system operated by fallible human beings. The question is always what can be done afterwards to right the situation? In Lumley's case, I can't see that there's anything you can do at the moment. I agree with Paul Maxted that you'd be unlikely to get much change out of the Court of Appeal. Your only realistic hope is that the police will arrest the others and more of the truth will emerge. Though whether that will assist Lumley is anyone's guess. Incidentally, where is he?'

'That's another thing,' Rosa said indignantly. 'Trying to find out which prison a client has been carted off to is like turning over stones in search of a rare species. The whole system's chaotic with prisons not knowing who they've got and who they haven't. Anyway, the answer to your question is Wandsworth, though it took me half a dozen calls to find out.'

'The odds are he'll be kept there several months before being moved.'

'I'm proposing to go and see him tomorrow afternoon,' she said, getting up from her chair. Giving her partner a disarming smile, she added, 'Sorry if I've gone on about Lumley, but thank you for listening to me, even if I can't follow your advice and "forget it".'

Wandsworth prison in south London housed a number of different categories of convicted men. For some it was a mere staging-post, for others it became a way of life. In common with most other prisons it was dangerously overcrowded.

The first time Rosa had become aware of its existence was when, as a child, she had heard two women on a bus talking about the execution of a notorious murderer that had been carried out there that morning. It had sent a chill down her spine and she was reminded of the conversation every time she visited one of her clients at the prison.

Looking neat and composed in his blue prison garb, Stephen Lumley entered the interview-room with a shy smile.

'I didn't expect to see you so soon,' he said.

'I thought I'd come and see how you were.'

'I've already been given my parole eligibility date. It's 10th June in two years' time. That means I've only got 728 more days to serve, which sounds much less than six years.'

'It *is* much less. Nowadays, you're eligible for parole after serving a third of your sentence. But maybe you won't be stuck inside even for as long as that.'

'How do you mean?' he asked eagerly.

'In the first place, Mr Maxted's considering whether we have grounds for appeal, though to be frank he's not too optimistic.'

His expression faded and he shook his head with a despondent air.

'Sometimes I still can't believe it's actually happened. I never thought an innocent person could be found guilty.' He gave Rosa an imploring look. 'How can it happen?'

'I'm afraid you're a victim of particularly cruel circumstances. It's because I believe in your innocence that I'm prepared to fight on.' She gave him a rueful smile. 'I still can't guarantee success, but I won't fail you for want of effort.' She paused. 'You're the first client to whom I've ever said that, namely that I believe in their innocence and I'm only saying it now as I hope it'll give you some sort of strength to face the future.' With an abrupt change of tone, she went on, 'Did you ever meet Les Fingle who once worked for your uncle?'

He frowned. 'Was he the bloke who got the push for dishonesty?'

'Yes.'

'I used to see him when I went to Firley Street. He was there quite some time, but I didn't know him outside the shop. Why do you want to know?'

Rosa decided that the moment had come to tell him of the Fingle angle.

'I never mentioned him before,' she said at the end, 'as there was nothing substantial to go on. There still isn't and, anyway, I've no idea how to get in touch with him. He fades in and out like a ghost, but I feel he has information about the robbery.'

'What information?' Lumley asked in a puzzled tone.

'I've no idea. Moreover, I do urge you not to build any hopes.'

'And you think he may make contact again?'

'It's possible. My guess is that he's been waiting for the end of the trial. If you'd been acquitted, I don't expect we'd ever hear from him again, but I'm hoping he'll realise your conviction is a miscarriage of justice and his conscience won't let him remain silent.'

He pulled a face and said sourly, 'The odds are he hasn't got one.'

'I don't believe he'd have proposed the Reading meeting if his conscience hadn't been nagging him.'

'More likely he just wanted to find out what you were up to.'

'I still believe I'm right.'

'You go a lot by instinct, don't you?' he said, as though it were a novel idea.

'I've learnt to trust my instinct and it doesn't often let me down.' She gave him a wry smile. 'It's my instinct that tells me you're innocent.' He clearly appreciated the comment and she went on, 'Have you applied for a job yet? It's better to be kept busy all day than shut up in a cell.'

He nodded. 'How long do you think I'll be here?'

'At a guess, anything between six and twelve months.'

'Where am I likely to go then?'

'To a category B closed prison. But my advice is to take each day as it comes.'

'By tomorrow I'll only have 727 more days.'

Les Fingle was worried, which was nothing new. The day after he met Rosa and Ben in Reading he moved again, this time to Oxford. He had no wish to return to London for a number of reasons, one being that he was anxious to break free from Renate's maternal embrace.

Oxford, like Brighton, was cosmopolitan with a large transient population of young people and that suited him.

His money was beginning to run short and he found himself a temporary job in a hamburger bar. Moreover, a girl he met on his first evening there offered to share her room with him. To her and to the manager of the hamburger bar he was Gary Fox.

He was paid only a pittance which was the manager's quid pro quo for not asking any awkward questions or seeking references. Les was prepared for this as he had no intention of staying very long. He just wanted time to sort out his thoughts and decide what to do.

He had read of Lumley's conviction and sentence in a newspaper. Armed robberies being so commonplace, it was only a brief item of news, but he had been looking out for it.

Meanwhile, he felt reasonably secure in Oxford and security was what he most needed. He had to decide whether to get in touch with Lumley's solicitor again, about which his feelings fluctuated. His mood tended to alternate between anger and anxiety. Anger at finding himself in a difficult position and anxiety as to the future.

He would give himself a bit longer to weigh up his options. To lie low and stay silent would be the course of self-interest and he didn't seriously pretend that he was motivated by anything else. Certainly his conscience did give him the occasional prick, but he was used to smothering it when it became too troublesome. On the other hand, a renewal of contact with Lumley's solicitor could also be seen as an act of self-interest, for he was still smarting from the series of misfortunes he'd suffered since being peremptorily sacked by Bernard Hammond. He had thought he was to have a satisfying moment of revenge, but even that had turned sour.

If only he could foresee clearly the consequences of further contact with Lumley's lawyer . . .

'What are you doing?'

Bernard Hammond started. He had not heard his wife come downstairs from the bedroom and turned his head to find her standing in the doorway of his study.

'Just paying some bills,' he said, pushing his cheque-book under a pile of papers.

'What bills?' she asked. 'I thought you'd done them all yesterday.'

'I'd overlooked one or two.'

She came further into the room. 'Which ones?'

'What's it matter which ones?' he said testily.

'I just wondered.'

'Well, stop wondering and fetch me a drink.'

She left the room and returned a little later with a Scotch and water. As she put the glass on his desk she contrived to sweep all the papers, including his cheque-book, on to the floor.

'Oh, how clumsy of me!' she exclaimed, as she quickly

bent down to pick them up. No additional sleight of hand was required to enable her to see a cheque for £250 made payable to Christine Lumley.

Her husband watched her while he waited for her comment.

'Conscience money, is it?' she enquired, sardonically.

'Don't be ridiculous! She must be having a hard time and I wanted to help her.'

'I can't see what she's done to deserve your help.'

'She's Stephen's wife and has two young children. I feel sorry for her despite the robbery.'

'Aren't you being rather naïve?'

'I don't think so.'

'Supposing it came out later that you were supporting her?'

'First of all, I can't see it coming out and secondly, even if it did, I hope it would be seen as a small act of charity and nothing more.' He paused. 'And thirdly, sending her a cheque for £250 can hardly be called supporting her.'

'As long as it's a one-off payment I don't suppose it is, but I'd advise you against sending her regular maintenance contributions.'

'Let's leave it at that, shall we?' he said frostily.

She bit her lip. 'OK, Bernard, so it's none of my business, but I still think it's unwise to keep in touch with the Lumleys. It could compromise you.'

He frowned. 'I fail to see how.'

'Supposing the police catch the other men?'

'I still don't follow you.'

'And they say that Stephen was behind the robbery.'

'He may have been part of it, but I'm certain he never organised it.'

'It doesn't matter whether he masterminded it or was merely a willing participant, it could still be embarrassing if it came out that you'd been secretly giving money to Stephen's wife.'

'I think you're making a mountain out of a molehill. Indeed, I don't think it's even a molehill.'

'If that's your view, why were you being so furtive about

sending Christine a cheque? You obviously didn't want me to know.'

'Give it a rest, Carol,' he said sharply. Then in a softer tone, 'Fetch me another drink and tell me what we're having for supper.'

'Chicken curry,' she replied, as she left the room.

He let out a sigh. He could not help remembering what excellent cooks his first two wives had been. Carol had many qualities, but cooking was not among them. Chicken curry meant soggy rice and a runny sauce poured over pieces of fowl. He knew that she was jealous of Stephen and his wife, despite his efforts to reassure her that she had no need to harbour such feelings. She knew that the bulk of his estate would come to her on his death and that Stephen and his children received only small legacies.

She returned to the room with his drink.

'Here you are,' she said, putting the glass down in front of him and kissing the top of his bald head. 'I'm sorry if I seemed to nag you. It's only because I love you very much that I sometimes get things out of perspective.'

He gave her hand an affectionate squeeze. 'I know,' he said gently. 'Tell you what, why don't we eat out tonight?'

It was a sultry afternoon and London was not the best place to be. Bernard Hammond's shop, with its absence of any air-conditioning apart from an ancient fan at one end of the counter, was particularly stuffy. Security required the door to be kept locked and only buzzed open when a customer looked safe to admit. And the fan merely stirred the air in its vicinity.

'I wish you'd tell him to get a proper fan,' Susan Cunliffe said, standing as close to it as she safely could.

'Tell him yourself,' Philip Wadingham replied.

It was not often that the two of them were left on their own in the shop, but the Hammonds had gone out just after three o'clock to see their solicitor. Ever since the robbery, they had been in dispute with their insurance company and the matter had now reached the hands of lawyers.

Carol Hammond had suggested that her husband should go on his own, leaving her to mind the shop, but he had insisted that she accompany him.

'We'll be back by four thirty,' he had said as they left.

'That's all right, Mr Hammond,' Wadingham had assured him. 'Susan and I can cope all right. Anyway, it looks like being a quiet afternoon.'

Philip Wadingham enjoyed his brief spells of authority and lost no opportunity to lord it over Susan.

'I'll get Miss Cunliffe to serve you, sir,' he would say, beckoning to Susan.

It was only three days since Lumley's trial had ended and it was still fresh in their minds. The result had been greeted with relief by everyone at the shop, apart from Susan who wasn't too sure what she felt.

'I keep on thinking about Stephen,' she remarked, as the minutes ticked slowly away that hot afternoon. 'I suppose he *was* guilty?'

'As guilty as hell,' Wadingham retorted in a superior sort of tone.

'I wish I could feel as certain . . . '

'If you're ever on a jury, everyone'll get off.'

'I still can't understand why he should have done it.'

'Money, of course.'

'But he was bound to be caught.'

'He was obviously driven by desperation. If you ask me, there's a share of the loot waiting for him when he comes out, provided he keeps his mouth shut about the other two.' With a slight note of triumph, he went on, 'Don't forget it was a majority verdict. There were two jurors who apparently swallowed his story, so he wasn't far off being acquitted. It only needed one more sucker on the jury for that to have happened.'

'I still find it very odd, the more so as time passes,' she said in a puzzled tone.

'Well, I suggest you keep your thoughts to yourself. The Hammonds wouldn't be very pleased to hear what you've been saying.'

'I've no intention of telling them,' she said indignantly.

'Good, I'm glad to hear it.'

'You really can sound smug, Philip,' she remarked, stung by his comment.

He gave a disdainful shrug. 'As far as I'm concerned, armed robbers belong behind bars and you won't catch me shedding any tears for Lumley.'

Susan had never particularly cared for Philip Wadingham, but he seemed to have become more insufferable since the robbery. And in the few days since the end of the trial, even more so.

Chapter 13

Tracy Wilkin turned the key and opened the door of her room. She expected to see Gary asleep on top of the bed. He usually took a nap in the afternoon when he was on late shift at the hamburger bar. But the room was empty.

She threw her duffel bag down on the divan and went across to the corner where an electric kettle, a jar of instant coffee and two mugs stood on a ledge. Both mugs were dirty and she rinsed one under the wash-basin tap. While she waited for the kettle to boil she ran her hands through her hair. It was an untidy mess, but she had grown used to it being that way. Secretly she thought the blown-haystack look rather suited her country girl appearance.

She was attending a secretarial college in north Oxford which expected its students to work hard or leave. She always brought back a considerable amount of homework which had to be done by the next day. As Gary wasn't there, she decided to get down to it straightaway. Possibly his work rota had been changed and he'd be back from the bar a little later, which would mean they could spend the evening together and go out for a drink in one of the pubs that abounded in the area.

She carried her mug of coffee across to the small cluttered table near the window and cleared a space. It was then she noticed he had left a note. 'Gone out. See you later', was all it said. As she sat down she saw that he had been writing a letter. She pulled the writing pad towards her and read with her curiosity aroused. As far as she was aware he hadn't written any letters during the week he had been living with her.

'Dear Ms Epton,' the letter ran, 'Meet me in the arrival hall of Terminal One at Heathrow on'

It was clear that he had been interrupted at that point, the inference being that he had gone out in a hurry. It was probable he had received a phone call. There was a pay-phone in the hall and she knew he had made a number of calls, because he had several times asked her for change. It was also possible that he had received calls. Whenever the phone rang, the person nearest to it usually answered, unless beaten to it by someone who was actually expecting a call.

She wondered who 'Ms Epton' was. Presumably not a girlfriend, addressed with such formality. Maybe he would tell her, but it wouldn't bother her if he didn't.

By the time she completed her homework it was five thirty and there was still no sign of Gary. Presumably he wouldn't now be back until after midnight when the hamburger bar closed.

After tidying the room up a bit and washing a pair of tights, she went downstairs and phoned a girl with whom she'd become friendly on the course.

'It's Tracy, Linda. Care to go out for a drink this evening?'

'Why not? Kurt's ditched me.'

'I thought he was supposed to be madly in love with you?'

'That's what I thought too. I'm livid. Will Gary be coming?'

'I've not seen him all afternoon. He left a note saying he'd gone out.'

'That's more than Kurt did. I only heard from one of his friends that he's gone up to London for the night. Well, he needn't bring his face round here again.'

'I expect you'll forgive him.'

'I expect I shall and that makes me even madder.'

In the event the girls passed an agreeable evening together, rejecting a number of attempts to pick them up. When they parted company Tracy decided to go to the hamburger bar and wait for Gary to finish work. Although they had known each other barely a week, she had come to like him quite a lot. He mayn't have been the best-looking boyfriend she'd ever had, nor yet the sexiest, but she was still happy to have him share her room for a while.

As she entered, she spotted the manager at the further end of the counter. She knew him to be a surly fellow who seldom smiled except at someone's expense.

'Is Gary about?' she enquired.

'No.'

'Hasn't he been here this evening?'

'No.'

'Do you know what's happened to him?'

'No. What's more you can tell him he's finished here as far as I'm concerned. I've no time for people who let me down.'

There seemed nothing further to be said and Tracy turned on her heel and left. As she made her lonely way home, she wondered what had happened to him. Maybe he was now back, but the room was as empty as when she had left it a few hours earlier and it was soon apparent that he hadn't returned during her absence.

She undressed quickly and went to bed. In the world of casual relationships which she frequented, she was used to people coming and going in her life without warning.

Nevertheless, there was something distinctly odd about Gary's disappearance. He hadn't taken anything with him and there was that unfinished letter to Ms Epton . . .

That was all on Monday and it was Thursday before Gary Fox, otherwise Les Fingle, reappeared. By then he had been dead for three days.

His body was discovered in the back of a car left in one of the city's multi-storey car parks. It was covered by a blanket and might have remained unnoticed for longer had not a drunken driver, returning from a midday celebration, reversed his own car into the rear of the other, causing one of Les's arms to become dislodged and swing free of the blanket. This had a rapidly sobering effect on the miscreant driver who lurched off to the attendant's kiosk to report his find.

Within fifteen minutes the police had arrived, though

there was then a further delay until a key was found which would open the car door.

A uniformed sergeant carefully lifted the blanket to reveal Les Fingle lying in a foetal position on the rear seat. Used as he was to sudden death, the Sergeant shrank back in revulsion when he observed Les's face. He had been strangled with a length of sash-cord which was embedded in his neck. The effects of that plus three days of warm weather made him a sight to repel even an experienced police officer.

He recovered himself quickly, however, and in next to no time an intensive murder enquiry was under way, with Detective Chief Inspector Becker in charge.

Before nightfall it had been established that the car (a Volvo) had been there since Monday evening, though none of the attendants had any clear recollection of its arrival or of the person driving it. One of them had noticed it on Tuesday morning for it stood alone on the top floor of the car park, which filled up as the morning went on. It was not exceptional for cars to be left for several days at a time and there was nothing about the Volvo, Becker was told, to arouse anyone's suspicions. He couldn't help feeling, however, that a bulky object covered by a blanket on the back seat might have caused someone to investigate rather sooner.

It was also established that the car had been stolen from a meter bay off the Earl's Court Road in west London some time during the previous weekend. To delay detection one of the registration digits had been changed from 0 to 8 and one of the letters from R to B. This had been sufficient to confuse the computer that logged details of stolen cars.

It was around three thirty in the afternoon when the body was discovered and the last edition of the *Oxford Mail* carried a brief report of the murder in its stop-press. It was mentioned that the dead man was thought to be in his early thirties but that the police had not yet identified him.

It was sufficient, however, to send Tracy, when she read it, hurrying to the pay-phone in the hall.

★ ★ ★

109

Tracy sat with a cup of hot sweet tea in front of her. She had just come from the mortuary where she had identified the body of the man she knew as Gary Fox. She was still feeling numbed with shock.

Detective Chief Inspector Becker observed her with a thoughtful expression as he awaited his moment.

'Feeling a bit better now?' he enquired in a sympathetic tone. She gave a small nod and he went on, 'We're grateful to you for coming forward so promptly, Miss Wilkin. By the way, mind if I call you Tracy, it's less of a mouthful? I'm afraid he wasn't a pleasant sight, but it was important to get him identified as soon as possible and so you've been a great help. You say you last saw him on Monday when you went off to your secretarial college?'

'Yes,' she said in a nervous whisper.

'And what time did you return?'

'Shortly before two o'clock.'

'And that was when you found the note he'd left you saying he'd gone out?' She nodded. 'It's a pity you destroyed it, but I realise you had no reason to keep it. Just tell me again exactly what it said.'

'"Have gone out. See you later."'

'Hmm. And then there was this letter he'd begun writing to a Ms Epton. Have you any idea who she is?'

'No.'

'He'd never mentioned her?'

'No.'

'Not to worry. With luck we'll be able to trace her.' He paused. 'How long exactly had you known Gary?'

'Just a week.'

'I think you said you met him in a café?'

'Yes.'

'What did he tell you about himself?'

She sipped her tea before replying.

'He said he'd arrived in Oxford that day and was looking for somewhere to stay.'

'And you told him he could share your room?'

'That was later after we'd been talking quite a long time.'

110

'Did he say where he'd come from?'

'I gathered from London.'

'And why he'd come to Oxford?'

'He didn't say.'

'Did you ever get the impression that he might be on the run from something?'

'You mean, that he was a criminal?'

'Not necessarily. Perhaps I should have said running away from something, rather than on the run.'

She gave him a solemn look.

'Don't we all spend our lives running away?'

'Yes ... Well ... I wouldn't know about that,' Becker said briskly. Operating in a university city had taught him that the most mundane police enquiry could become the subject of philosophical debate, if you didn't watch out. He got up. 'If you're ready, I'll get a car to take us to your address. I'd like to have a look through Gary's belongings. We'll go in an unmarked car as I don't wish to give your neighbours anything to talk about.'

The house in which she lived lay in one of the residential streets of north Oxford. Tracy led the way upstairs. There didn't appear to be anyone else about and Becker assumed that the occupants of the other rooms were still at their places of work.

Her room gave the impression of bed-sitter land at its most functional. A rumpled duvet on the bed looked like a relief map of the Himalayas and articles of clothing were scattered around as though deposited by a high wind. She pointed at a suitcase that lay on the floor to one side of the divan.

'That's all he brought,' she said.

Becker knelt down and lifted the lid which was being kept open by a pair of socks hanging out. The case revealed a jumble of clothes.

'Have you been through this lot?' he enquired, and when she shook her head, added incredulously, 'Not at all?'

'No. It would have been invading his privacy.' She managed somehow to divest the remark of any priggish overtones.

He pulled out a pair of jeans and went through the pockets, finding nothing apart from a bus ticket, which he carefully scrutinised.

'Did he ever mention Reading?' he asked.

'No.'

'This is a Reading bus ticket,' he explained.

'I'm afraid I can't help.'

After a further rummage, he extracted a creased brown envelope and shook the contents on to the floor.

'Ha!' he exclaimed as he held up a driving licence in a plastic holder. 'It's in the name of Leslie Frank Fingle. Ever heard of him?'

'No.'

'Either it's stolen or Gary Fox and Leslie Fingle are the same person. Born 18th August, 1956,' he read out. 'That would make him thirty-three this year which is about right for the chap in the mortuary. The licence gives his address as forty-two Pilatus Road, Watford, but that was ten years ago and I imagine he's had a few changes of address since then without notifying the DVLC.' He picked up two further documents from the floor and examined them. 'His National Insurance Card and Medical Record Card are also in the name of Fingle, so I reckon that's who he is – or was. I wonder why he assumed a false name,' he went on in a speculative tone. He put his hand in his pocket and pulled out the unfinished letter to Rosa which Tracy had given him. 'Maybe Ms Epton will have answers to all my questions. Somehow I must find her.' In a musing sort of voice, he added, 'I suppose the arrival hall of Heathrow's Terminal One is as anonymous a meeting place as any. But what was to be the purpose of their meeting?' He gave Tracy a small smile. 'Think you'd like to join the police?'

Chapter 14

Becker had begun to think that everything was being served up to him on a plate, for not only had he established the identity of the dead man more easily than he might have expected, but he had hardly returned to the station when a recently transferred officer knocked on his door.

'I've heard a buzz, sir, that you're trying to trace a Miss Epton?'

'Yes, do you know the name?'

'She's a London solicitor. I met her on a case when I was stationed at Ealing. Her name's Rosa Epton and she's a pretty nimble defence lawyer. I don't know if she's the person you're looking for.'

'I'll soon find out. Meanwhile, thanks a lot. Any idea where her office is?'

'I think it was somewhere in the Hammersmith area.'

'Probably still is. Thanks again. I'll let you know if she proves to be the person I want to track down.'

It wasn't long before Becker had found Rosa's name amongst the listed London solicitors and that she was with the firm of Snaith and Epton.

'Please let my luck hold,' he murmured to himself as he put through a call. Even so, he was half-ready to be told that Miss Epton had left for Patagonia that very morning. Luck could abruptly run out.

'Miss Epton?' he said eagerly, on discovering that she was actually in her office. 'This is Detective Chief Inspector Becker of Thames Valley Police at Oxford. I have a murder enquiry on my hands and I'm wondering if the name Leslie Fingle means anything to you?'

'It certainly does. I've been hoping he'd get in touch with me. Why?'

'I'm afraid he's dead.'

'Murdered?'

'Yes.'

'Can you tell me what happened?'

'It seems to me, Miss Epton, that we each have information the other would like. I suggest we meet.'

Thus it was that Rosa caught a train to Oxford first thing the next morning and Detective Chief Inspector Becker met her at the station.

After Rosa had related how she had become involved with Fingle, Becker responded by giving her details of the murder.

'It confirms my belief that he was killed to keep his mouth shut,' Rosa said when Becker finished. 'I know it sounds a cliché, but I'm sure that's what has happened. And if you want further confirmation, there's the letter he'd begun to me. I'm convinced he was ready to provide me with information which would help to prove Lumley's innocence. He'd been waiting to see the result of the trial.'

'You make it sound very plausible, Miss Epton. But will Inspector Cleave see it in the same way?'

'He's so certain my client is guilty that it colours his judgment,' Rosa observed.

'And, of course, he may be right. After all, the jury's verdict supports his view.'

'He's not right and the jury's verdict was a miscarriage of justice,' Rosa declared firmly.

'Assuming for a moment that you are right, tell me how you see the scenario of Fingle's death?'

'In the first place, he was obviously in on the robbery, though I doubt whether he was one of the men who carried it out . . .'

'Could he not have been the driver of the getaway car?'

'I hadn't thought of that. It's certainly a possibility.'

'If so, he'd have known who the robbers were. He may

114

even have supplied the know-how, seeing that he had once worked at Hammond's.'

Rosa nodded keenly. 'And then afterwards the thieves fell out as so often happens, probably over a division of the spoil and Fingle became the disgruntled odd man out. It must have been about the time that Ben, our clerk, ran him to earth and managed to nudge his conscience into action.'

'More likely, made him see how he could bring a bit of pressure to bear on those who'd cheated him. He doesn't sound the sort of person to have had a conscience.'

'Perhaps I have more faith in human nature.'

Becker smiled. 'I have more than you might expect to find in someone who's been a policeman for twenty-two years. Anyway, go on with what you were saying.'

'I suspect that Fingle may have been ready to talk when we met at Reading, but then held back at the last moment.'

'We know from Tracy Wilkin that he arrived in Oxford a day or so after seeing you, by which time he'd become Gary Fox.'

'He obviously knew he was running risks and decided to conceal his identity.'

'And yet he must have got in touch with his murderer and told him where he was. Why'd he do that if he didn't want to be found?'

'He could have been motivated by fear and greed at the same time. If I'm right, he must have threatened the perpetrators of the robbery with exposure.'

'In that event, he seriously overestimated his skills.'

'He mayn't have believed his life would actually be in danger.'

'The use of a gun at the shop should have told him he wasn't playing with kids.' Becker paused. 'I'm not saying you're wrong, Miss Epton, but not everything fits quite as neatly as you choose to believe. After all, it could only have been Fingle himself who invited his murderer to meet him in Oxford. If so, he really was sticking out his neck.'

'Presumably he believed he could handle the situation. Greed overcame fear.'

Becker sighed. 'Well, I'm most grateful to you, Miss Epton. Even if you've not solved the murder for me, you've provided some very valuable background information. I'll obviously need to get in touch with Inspector Cleave.'

Rosa wasn't long out of the building before Becker was putting through a call to London. After introducing himself, he explained his reason for phoning while Cleave listened in silence.

'I'd be interested to hear what you think of Miss Epton's views,' he said at the end.

Cleave gave a small, hollow laugh.

'One has to hand it to her, she's a real fighter who never gives up. But don't let her fool you about Lumley being innocent. The jury found him guilty and it'd have been a bloody scandal if they hadn't.'

'Did you ever uncover any evidence of Fingle's involvement in the robbery?'

'None. To be honest, I wasn't interested in disgruntled ex-Hammond employees. For all I know, there could have been dozens of them. Lumley was caught red-handed and we focused all our attention on him. I'm darned certain he could give us the names of the others if he wanted to. Presumably it suits him to stay silent. He'll serve his sentence, or what there is of it with all the reductions they get these days, then come out and live happily ever after.' Cleave paused. 'As a matter of fact I've recently learnt that his wife has been receiving mysterious sums of money and there's not much doubt where that's coming from.'

'Do you hold out any hope of identifying the others involved in the robbery?'

'Not without a tip-off and it's getting a bit late for that. You know how it is, sometimes you're swamped with information, other times all sources seem to have dried up. It certainly hasn't been for want of trying, I assure you of that.' His tone was such as to defy any argument.

Becker was aware of the delicacy of the situation. Cleave had shown no inclination to jump up and down with joy at what he'd been told. Rosa Epton had warned that he would take a lot of convincing and that now appeared to be an understatement.

'Well, I'll keep in touch with you, Inspector,' Becker said affably. 'It's been useful talking things over with you.'

'Hope you catch your murderer,' Cleave replied in like tone.

Becker had nothing against his opposite number in London, but it was a fact of life that the Met had always regarded themselves as innately superior to their brethren in provincial forces. It might have been so once, but not now. Big was no longer best. Nevertheless, the Met still contrived to retain its image of superiority, even if the days had passed when county chief constables used to 'call in the Yard' to help solve their more difficult crimes. The image was now sustained by news items about senior Scotland Yard officers jetting off to foreign parts at the request of some government or another.

Becker was reflecting on this when one of his detective sergeants burst into his room.

'They've found a thumbprint on the roll of Polo mints that was in the car, sir. It's that of a man named Lee Harrison who has a record of burglaries and the odd spot of violence. Hence his prints are on the computer. I've checked with the owner of the car, sir,' he went on eagerly, 'and he says there was an unopened roll of Polo mints in the car when it was stolen. Obviously Harrison helped himself and removed his gloves to open them. It explains why there were no other prints in the car apart from the owner's. But I defy anyone to open a roll of mints with gloves on . . . '

'Yes, OK, Brian, I get your point, but where can we find this Harrison chap?'

'According to records, sir, he lives at forty-two Pilatus Road, Watford.'

Becker's head jerked back as if he'd received an uppercut to the chin.

'That's the address shown on Fingle's driving licence,' he said in a deeply thoughtful tone.

Chapter 15

Rosa paused for a minute on the pavement outside the police station, deciding what to do next. The options were to take an immediate train back to London or to hang around in the hope of seeing Tracy Wilkin when she came home from her secretarial course. Chief Inspector Becker had mentioned that she usually returned just before two o'clock. It was now noon. It didn't take Rosa more than a few seconds to make up her mind. She would find a café and have something to eat as she was feeling distinctly hungry. First, however, she would call her office and make sure there was nothing requiring her urgent attention.

The phone was answered by Ben who often relieved Stephanie for short spells at the switchboard.

'Hello, Miss E,' he said cheerfully, 'enjoying your day out?'

'Yes, thank you, Ben,' she replied crisply, 'and unless I'm wanted I don't propose to come in this afternoon. I'm in court tomorrow morning, so I'll pick up the papers I need on my way.'

'Like me to drop them round at your flat this evening?'

'Won't that be a nuisance?'

'No problem. And you needn't worry, I won't bring Lucy. She's got an evening class.'

'What course is she taking?'

'Cooking,' Ben said rather less cheerfully. 'She thinks it'll help get me to the altar. I tell her she's wasting her time, we've got a Chinese takeaway next door and a place that serves breakfast all day just along the street. By the way, Miss E, I almost forgot to tell you, Mr Chen phoned this

118

morning. He told Steph he'd tried to call you at home last night, but there was no reply and he wanted to make sure you were OK. Steph told him you'd gone to Oxford on a case.'

'Oh, well, if he calls me at home this evening, I'll be there,' Rosa remarked in a carefully casual tone.

During the seven months he had now been in Hong Kong, he had been phoning her regularly twice a week, not to mention making a flying visit to London at Easter. When they last spoke she had forgotten to tell him she was going to the theatre with friends the previous evening and it had obviously worried him not getting a reply. She missed him very much and there had been times during the Lumley case when she had longed to have him at hand. He was now due back in about six weeks and she looked forward eagerly to their reunion.

She found a pleasant-looking café and ordered a cottage cheese sandwich and a cup of black coffee. She lingered so long over her meal that the proprietor began to cast her suspicious glances. He probably thought she was waiting to slip out without paying when he was busy with other customers. It was one thirty and she decided to put his mind at rest.

Fifteen minutes later she turned into the street where Tracy Wilkin lived. She had just reached the house when she heard hurrying footsteps behind her. A girl with a wind-blown appearance and carrying a duffel bag passed her and scurried up the short path to the front door.

'Excuse me,' Rosa called out. 'Are you Tracy Wilkin?'

The girl halted and looked round. 'Yes,' she said. 'What do you want?'

Over the years Rosa felt she had acquired all the techniques of a quick-talking doorstep canvasser. It was an art that enabled her to explain herself coherently and succinctly.

'You'd better come in,' Tracy said when she finished.

Rosa followed her through the front door and up the stairs.

'Like a cup of tea or coffee?' Tracy asked when they were in her room.

'Thank you. Whichever's easier.'

119

'I always have tea when I get back.'

'That'll be fine.' While the kettle was boiling, Rosa went on, 'I know you must be fed up with answering questions about Les Fingle, but I'm wondering if anything I've told you has jogged your memory. When Chief Inspector Becker interviewed you, he wasn't aware of half the implications. For a start, he knew nothing about my client.'

'As a matter of fact there is something,' Tracy said. 'This robbery you've mentioned took place in Firley Street?'

'Yes. Hammond's, the jewellers.'

'It was Wednesday last week when I got back from college at about this same time. Gary was on the phone downstairs in the hall. He sounded angry and I heard him say something like, "I've never been properly paid for the Firley Street job." I went past him and came upstairs and as I reached the landing, he said, "Well, somebody had better pull their finger out or be ready for a showdown." I hadn't long been in the room before he came in.'

'Did he refer to his telephone conversation?'

'No.'

'Did you ask him about it?'

'No, it wasn't any of my business.'

'Maybe you speculated what he'd been talking about?'

'Not really. I imagined it was some job he'd done for which he hadn't been paid.'

'Did it occur to you that "job" might refer to some criminal undertaking?'

'No, why should it?'

'I just wondered,' Rosa said a trifle defensively.

'Gary had made it clear from the outset that he didn't welcome questions about himself and I accepted it. It wasn't as if we were embarking on some research project to find out what made each of us tick. It was only a casual relationship.' She gave a sudden convulsive shudder. 'I keep on seeing his face with those horrible marks round his neck. I don't feel I'll ever forget the sight of him in a mortuary drawer.'

'It must have been very unnerving.'

'One sees so many gruesome sights on the box that one

thinks one's hardened, but the real thing is quite different.'

Rosa nodded sympathetically. 'The more so when it's someone you've known.'

'Poor Gary. I wish our paths had never crossed.'

A few minutes later Rosa got up to go.

'Thank you for talking to me,' she said. 'And here's my card if you want to get in touch.'

She walked to the end of the road where she caught a bus into the city centre. From there it was only a short walk to the railway station.

Chief Inspector Becker had shown her Fingle's driving licence with the Watford address. This she had memorised and subsequently written down in the small notebook she always carried in her handbag.

That had been, of course, before Pilatus Road, Watford had also come up as the address of Fingle's potential murderer.

Chapter 16

Rosa had been home just over an hour when the entryphone gave its quavering buzz and Ben announced his arrival to an accompaniment of painful crackles. A couple of minutes later he appeared at her flat door.

'I've brought your court papers for tomorrow,' he said, handing her a buff file.

'Thanks, Ben. That's a great help. Would you like a drink?'

'I wouldn't say no, Miss E,' he said, still puffing from climbing the stairs to the third floor. 'Don't you mind not having a lift?'

'I'm used to it. Anyway, I look upon the stairs as part of my daily exercise. You shouldn't get out of breath at your age.'

'I reckon I'm pretty fit, but there's something about stairs . . .'

Rosa smiled. 'Well, come in and have a rest before the return journey. What would you like?'

'A beer would be smashing.'

He stood in the doorway of her tiny kitchen and watched her take a can of Carlsberg lager from the fridge, which she handed him together with a glass.

'You'd better open it. I always get it all over me.'

He grinned, revealing two rows of even white teeth through the carefully cultivated stubble he had recently grown.

'Lucy still likes your designer stubble, does she?' Rosa said with a quizzical smile.

Ben's grin widened. 'Seems to,' he replied complacently. Following her into the living-room, he went on, 'How was your trip to Oxford? Did you find out anything that helps our bloke?'

'I'm not sure yet,' she said and went on to tell him of her talk with Chief Inspector Becker and her subsequent visit to Tracy Wilkin.

'Obviously Fingle's murderer knew he was about to grass. The letter he was writing you shows that.'

'I don't think the murderer can have known he was in the act of writing to me. More likely it was what Fingle had threatened to do if he didn't receive his pay-off. I doubt whether my name came into it; he probably threatened to go to the police.'

Ben assumed a frowning air. 'You don't think the murderer went to the room and saw the letter lying there?'

'No. I think it's much more likely that Fingle met his murderer somewhere in the city and that they drove out to a secluded spot in the countryside to argue the toss. The other man had come prepared for every eventuality, including murder. After killing Fingle, he covered the body with a blanket and drove back into the city, leaving the car where it was discovered a few days later. He probably reckoned – and rightly so as things turned out – that it would arouse less suspicion in a multi-storey car park than if left at the roadside.'

Ben gave an intent nod. 'So what's next on the agenda?' he enquired.

'If I can get away from the office a bit early tomorrow afternoon, I'd like you to accompany me on a trip to Watford. It may be a waste of time, but I want to take a look at forty-two Pilatus Road.'

Ben's face lit up. 'Sure, we'll sus it out.' After a pause he added, 'Where the hell did it get a name like that?'

'There's a Mount Pilatus near Lucerne in Switzerland. That's the only Pilatus I know.'

'Thought it might have something to do with Pontius Pilate. He was a pretty murderous bloke, wasn't he?'

Rosa laughed. 'Well, if we can both be spared from the office, we'll set off around three thirty.'

'Have you heard anything recent from Lumley himself?'

'No, I've been waiting to go and visit him until I had something worth saying.'

'What about Mrs Lumley? I'd expected her to be ringing up every other day.'

'I'm glad she hasn't,' Rosa said in a reflective tone.

'You still believe Lumley's innocent, don't you, Miss E?'

'I wouldn't be doing all this unpaid running around if I didn't,' she said.

Though Pilatus Road was neither scenic nor in any way suggestive of Switzerland, it was quite different from Rosa's expectations. She thought they would find a terraced street of Victorian villas; instead there were modern bungalows with trim gardens and carefully spaced acacia trees lining the road. Many of the bungalows bore names such as 'Sorrento', 'Mykonos' and 'Algarve', even 'Seychelles' which suggested one-upmanship. Number forty-two, however, had no name, only the figures 42 fixed to a wooden gate.

As they walked up the short path to the front door, Rosa noticed a lace curtain being delicately pulled aside in one of the windows of the bungalow next door, which was number forty. A pale female face peered at them, but withdrew abruptly when Rosa met its enquiring gaze.

Although a bright summer's afternoon, all the curtains at number forty-two were drawn across the windows.

'Doesn't look as if there's anyone at home,' Ben remarked, a fact which was confirmed when the door remained unanswered despite persistent ringing of the bell and a barrage of knocks from Ben's knuckles.

'Let's have a look round the back,' Rosa said.

A cement path ran round the side of the bungalow to a paved patio at the back on which were set out some ancient items of garden furniture.

'Reckon they got that lot off some dump,' Ben commented.

The windows on this side of the bungalow also had curtains drawn across them.

'I suppose they could be on holiday,' Rosa said in a doubtful tone.

For a few seconds they gazed across an unkempt stretch of grass, which was lined by unweeded flower-beds, towards a vegetable patch at the bottom of the garden.

'Obviously not keen gardeners,' Ben remarked. 'Probably too busy, planning robberies and things.'

'The thing is who are *they*?'

As they retraced their steps round the side of the bungalow, a side door in number forty opened and the owner of the pale face and interested gaze appeared. She gave a delicate cough.

'I'm afraid you won't find anyone at home. If you care to come round to my door, perhaps I can help you.' The voice was genteel and redolent of lavender sachets and home-knitted angora-wool bed-jackets.

She was waiting for them at her open front door and Rosa's impression was fortified of someone who had been told as a child what a dainty little thing she was and who had been living up to the description ever since. Rosa guessed that she was now in her mid-fifties. Her complexion was pale but flawless and she had carefully set golden hair which she gently patted as they approached.

'Are you from television or a newspaper?' she enquired in a distinctly hopeful tone as they reached her doorstep.

'No,' Rosa said, taken aback by the question. 'Neither.'

'Not the police again?' the woman went on before Rosa could introduce herself.

'No, my name's Rosa Epton and I'm a solicitor. This is my assistant, Mr Stocker. May we come in?'

Ben gave an embarrassed grin, being unused to such a formal introduction.

'I'm afraid I don't know your name,' Rosa went on as she stepped inside.

'Miss Gamley. Miss Flora Gamley.' She led the way into the front room which was overpacked with furniture and contained enough bric-à-brac to keep a street stall in business for weeks. Perching herself on the edge of an uncomfortable-looking chair, Miss Gamley said, 'Please be seated,' rather as if she was graciously pleased to grant an audience.

'Do I gather from what you said, Miss Gamley, that the police have already been making enquiries next door?'

'They were there for several hours yesterday evening. They had to force an entry as Mr and Mrs Harrison had gone away. It was most alarming, but then a charming young officer came to my door to allay my fears and assure me they were genuine policemen.'

'Did he tell you what they were after?'

Miss Gamley gave a portentous nod. 'There's been a murder and they wanted to interview Mr Harrison. I was able to tell them that Mr and Mrs Harrison had gone away a few days ago.'

'How long had the Harrisons lived there?' Rosa enquired, hoping for enlightenment as to how they fitted in to her research.

'Quite a long time,' Miss Gamley said, less than helpfully. 'They kept themselves to themselves and nobody knew much about them. Mrs Unwin who lived in the bungalow on the other side used to say she was sure that Mr Harrison worked in one of the government's secret departments. He never talked about his work, but one couldn't help noticing that sometimes he would not get home until the early hours.'

'Did his wife work?'

'I believe she had a jewellery stall in some market or other, but I never found out where.'

Nevertheless, it was an item of information that Rosa found interesting. She wondered what were Mrs Harrison's sources of supply. As for Mr Harrison, it was understandable that he would prefer to keep his neighbours in the dark as to whether he was a secret agent on government service or more profitably engaged in full-time burglary.

Miss Gamley gave her visitors a coy smile. 'May I ask what your interest is in Mr and Mrs Harrison?'

'I'm really trying to find out about someone named Leslie Fingle who once lived at forty-two Pilatus Road. Does the name mean anything to you?'

Miss Gamley frowned (even her frowns were delicately expressed) and slowly shook her head.

'I've never heard of such a person. Are you sure he lived there?'

'It's the address that appears on his driving licence.'

'How very strange! Now wait a moment . . . ' She looked suddenly thoughtful. 'I seem to remember there was a young man living there soon after the Harrisons moved in. I never knew his name and he didn't stay more than a few months. Mrs Unwin told me he was a distant relative of Mr Harrison.' Her mouth turned down in disapproval. 'Mrs Unwin is, I'm afraid, a bit of a busybody.' Rosa thought she detected a faint note of jealousy mingled with the self-righteousness. Nevertheless a visit to the omniscient Mrs Unwin might prove worthwhile. As if Miss Gamley read her thoughts, she said, 'Poor Mrs Unwin is in hospital at the moment and I don't know whether we'll see her again. She's very poorly.' She gave her forehead a delicate tap. 'And her mind's started to go as well.'

Rosa made a sympathetic sound. 'How old would this young man have been when he was staying with the Harrisons?'

'In his early twenties, I would think, but I'm not very good at guessing ages.'

Rosa reached into her bag and produced the newspaper photograph of Fingle which had appeared in the local press after his death when the police were still seeking to identify him. It had been touched up so as not to offend the susceptibilities of the paper's readers, but the likeness was there for anyone who had known him.

'Could this have been the young man?' Rosa asked, handing the cutting to Miss Gamley who gingerly peered at it.

'Yes, I can see a resemblance,' she said, 'though he was much fitter-looking in those days. He really doesn't look at all well in this photograph.'

'That's understandable. He was dead.'

Miss Gamley's hand shot up to her mouth in a theatrical gesture of horror.

'Oh, how dreadful! Is that why the police have been making enquiries next door?'

'Yes.'

'How unfortunate it should happen when the Harrisons have gone away!'

Rosa nodded. There was no point in sowing further seeds of worry in Miss Gamley's mind. It was better she should believe that the Harrisons' departure and Fingle's death were unconnected events. Maybe they were, though it seemed increasingly unlikely.

'I know one thing,' Ben observed as they drove back into town. 'I wouldn't want to have an old biddy like that for a neighbour. Give her half a chance and she'd know every time you went to the loo.'

'On the other hand, nosey neighbours can be a boon to society at large,' Rosa remarked. 'They're rather like spiders. Nobody loves them, but they serve a useful purpose.' In a thoughtful tone she went on, 'I wonder what Mr Harrison could tell us about the Firley Street robbery if he chose to speak.'

Chapter 17

The next day Rosa tried to call Christine Lumley a couple of times on her re-connected phone, but on neither occasion was there any reply. She hoped it didn't presage bad news. In any event she had made up her mind to visit Stephen Lumley the following day. She phoned the prison to advise them she was coming. If she was lucky, this would mean she wouldn't have to sit around waiting while he was fetched from some working party in a remote quarter of the prison.

She arrived in mid-afternoon and passed through the various security checks before reaching one of the legal interview-rooms.

'Come to see Lumley, have you?' an officer said conversationally as he unlocked a door for her.

'Yes, that's right.'

'He doesn't seem to have settled at all. Just frets all day. I was on duty on his landing last week and was telling him to snap out of it. Isn't doing himself any good.'

'I imagine he's not the only one in that state.'

'Except in his case, it seems more chronic. It's a bad state to get into. Everyone has fits of depression, that's only natural, but Lumley could become a mental case if he's not careful.'

'Has he seen the doctor?'

'Nothing much any doctor can do for him, except put him on some drug or another. It's all up to him.'

'He was convicted of a crime he didn't commit. Small wonder he's in a depressed state.'

'Yes, I've heard all that before,' the officer said in a

matter-of-fact tone. 'But what I know is that the best way of getting through a sentence and coming out sane the other end is to abide by the rules and keep as mentally and physically active as possible. OK, it's not as easy as it sounds with all the overcrowding and other problems, but there's something else I can tell you: life inside isn't nearly as soul-destroying as when I began my service. In those days cons weren't sent to prison as a punishment, but for punishment. Penal servitude it used to be called and that just about described it.' He let out a reflective sigh and pushed back his cap to scratch his cropped, grizzled head. 'Anyway, it's no skin off my nose, I retire at the end of the month. Whatever the public may think of us, we're not just a bunch of uncaring zombies. Would that we had the resources to do more.' He motioned Rosa to go on her way.

After what she had just heard she was relieved to find Lumley looking reasonably composed and alert when he came into the interview-room. He was freshly shaved, which she always regarded as a sign of a man's self-respect being intact.

He gave her a wan smile and sat down on the other side of the table.

'I tried to phone Christine yesterday, but couldn't get any reply,' Rosa said by way of opening the conversation.

'She's taken a couple of part-time jobs, so she's out quite a lot.'

'What about the children?'

'A near neighbour looks after them when they get out of school until Christine collects them. Two evenings a week a young girl babysits while she goes and works in the kitchen of a restaurant in Hampstead. It's not much money, but it helps.' He gave a shrug. 'I'd sooner she didn't, but I'm hardly in a position to give her orders.'

'Does she still visit you?'

'Yes,' he said, biting his lip, 'though I'm only allowed one social visit a month. And she was never much of a letter-writer.'

'Well, that all sounds as satisfactory as it can be,' Rosa remarked in a not altogether convincing tone.

'I've been hoping you'd come,' Lumley said, displaying a note of eagerness. 'I read about Fingle's murder in the paper. Where does that take us?'

Rosa told him of her visits to Oxford and Watford while he listened intently, his eyes never leaving her face.

'So the one person who could prove my innocence is dead,' he said bleakly when she finished.

'We don't know for certain that he could have proved you innocent—'

'His unfinished letter to you is good enough evidence for me,' he broke in.

'The important thing is that the ice has begun to crack. Fingle's murder and the Firley Street robbery must be connected, even if Inspector Cleave won't be easily persuaded. But the Oxford police have a murder enquiry on their hands and Chief Inspector Becker will be all out to make an arrest. Does Lee Harrison's name ring any bells with you?'

'I've never heard of him.'

'We must hope the police track him down. If I managed to get hold of a photograph of him, do you think you might recognise him as one of the Firley Street robbers?'

'I suppose I might,' he said doubtfully. 'Though all I recall about them is their obvious wigs and false moustaches. Anyway, how can you get hold of a photograph?'

'I haven't thought that out yet. Possibly I can't.'

'You could arrange a burglary at the bungalow.'

'Too risky. In any event, I doubt whether he's the sort of person to leave photographs of himself lying around. Particularly if he's done a permanent bunk.'

'Do you believe Fingle set the robbery up and got this Harrison bloke and a mate to carry it out?'

'But I don't understand why he should have waited so long to take his revenge on your uncle,' Rosa said in a puzzled tone. 'Moreover, robbery's not normally a crime of revenge. Malicious damage and arson, yes.'

'The longer he waited, the less likely he'd be to fall under suspicion.'

'There must be more to it than that,' Rosa observed with a distracted frown. 'There are still some missing pieces to the puzzle.'

She glanced up in time to catch the strangely mask-like expression on Lumley's face.

It was an expression that remained in her mind as she drove away from the prison. She wondered if she was being manipulated. By the time she reached her office, however, she had persuaded herself that this was an unworthy thought. She shouldn't be influenced by something as ephemeral as an expression; particularly an expression on the face of somebody under great mental and emotional strain.

She hoped his marriage would survive the enormous pressure now placed on it, but she would no longer take a bet on it. All the more reason for her to remain committed to his cause. Whatever the outcome, she must fight on.

Chapter 18

To the clinical observer Becker and Cleave were like two recently introduced cats, the one (Becker) seeking to make friendly advances, the other wary and uninterested.

As soon as the thumbprint on the roll of Polo mints was identified as that of Harrison whose address was the same as the one shown on Fingle's driving licence, Becker put through a second call to Cleave.

'Never heard of him,' Cleave said when Becker mentioned Harrison's name. 'I'm not saying he couldn't have been one of the Firley Street robbers, but then so might a million other people. Anyway, Watford's not in the Met, it comes under Hertfordshire. You'd better get in touch with them.'

Becker did so and an hour later was on his way to Pilatus Road, accompanied by Detective Sergeant Gillam. There they were met by two officers of the local CID, Detective Inspector Halford and Detective Constable Cash.

'The bungalow's deserted,' Halford said after introductions had been made. 'Seems the Harrisons took off four days ago. I made a few quick enquiries after you called. Gather they've lived here about nine years. No children and a marked disinclination to get involved with other residents. Harrison drove a large Jag and his wife a Renault hatchback. Both cars have also gone. Here are their registration numbers.' He handed Becker a slip of paper and went on, 'They've not come to our notice since they've lived here and nobody seems to know what Harrison did for a living. His wife had a jewellery stall in a street market. Probably an outlet for stolen goods.' He glanced across at the bungalow. 'Reckon it's more than trebled its value in the time they've been here,' he remarked in brisk telegraphese. 'Got a record, has he?'

Becker nodded. 'Yes, but nothing recent. He spent most of his early twenties in prison and he's now thirty-eight. He's either gone straight or undetected.'

'Don't ask me to guess which,' Halford remarked, giving the bungalow an appraising stare. 'Why don't we take a look inside. No point in being squeamish about search warrants and the like.'

Followed by Becker and the other two officers, they made their way round the side of the bungalow to the back, their progress closely monitored by Miss Gamley next door.

'Don't worry about her,' Halford said, flicking his head in her direction. 'DC Cash had a word with her before you came and told her we were police.' They reached a path that ran up the further side of the bungalow. 'Let's try here,' he said pausing before a frosted glass window. 'Almost certainly the bathroom. Also the neighbour on this side is in hospital, so unless the other old girl has X-ray eyes she won't see what we're up to.' He turned to the young DC with him. 'Go on, Colin, let's see you get that window open. And don't damage it more than you have to or the repairs'll come out of your pay packet.'

Under the watchful eyes of the other three, the hapless DC Cash, who was armed with a wrench, set about prising the window open.

'You'll never make a decent burglar, that's for sure,' Halford muttered impatiently. 'Wouldn't even have given you a tin of sardines to open if I'd known.'

Suddenly there was a sharp crack and a splintering of glass.

'At last,' Halford remarked. 'In you go and then you can unlock the kitchen door on the other side from here. We'll wait until you come back and report.'

With a bit of assistance from Detective Sergeant Gillam, DC Cash clambered through the window and disappeared.

DI Halford gave Becker a smile. 'He's a good lad, but it doesn't do to let them know.'

In what seemed like no time at all, Cash was back at the window.

'I'm afraid I can't open either the kitchen or the front door, sir. They're both fitted with mortice locks and there are no keys on the inside.'

'Hell!' Halford muttered crossly. Then turning to Becker, he said with a grin, 'After you, Chief Inspector.'

Following a somewhat undignified entry into the bungalow's bathroom, they stood for a moment regaining their breath.

'Not a toothbrush in sight,' Becker observed.

'I imagine you want the place gone over for fingerprints?' Halford said.

Becker nodded. 'A thumbprint matching the one on the Polo mints would be a very useful bit of evidence.'

'Shall I go round and draw back the curtains?' Cash asked from the doorway.

'Better not,' Halford said. 'Somebody might see us moving around and send for the police. We can turn lights on and off as we go.'

Although only just after eight on a pleasant summer's evening, the light indoors was minimal, for thick, heavy curtains hung across all the windows, save those in the kitchen and bathroom where slatted blinds kept prying eyes from gazing in.

A room by room examination of the premises produced no dramatic revelations. The lounge had a mint green carpet and a three-seat sofa in a darker shade of green with two matching easy chairs. There was a glass-topped coffee table with nothing on it and a large television set in one corner with items of hi-fi equipment next to it.

Whatever personal touches the room might once have displayed had seemingly been erased. There were neither books, pictures nor ornaments to reveal the occupants' taste. And the telephone on a table near the door had been unplugged.

'What do you make of it, Chief Inspector?' Halford asked.

'That they've done a bunk and stripped the place of any-thing that might put us on their trail. Let's take a look at the other rooms.'

Of these, one was totally bare of furniture, another appeared to be a store-room being full of cartons and packing-cases. The third was a bedroom with a king-size bed that virtually covered the floor space. There was a shaggy white carpet and a black ceiling adorned with silver moons and stars.

Becker slid back the doors of a built-in wardrobe which ran the length of one wall. A number of dresses hung at one end and various items of male clothing at the other. In between dangled a dozen loose coat-hangers.

'It's my guess they have another home somewhere,' Becker observed. 'They could be hiding out there. If they'd flown the country I wouldn't have expected them to take so much with them.'

'Could be you're right,' Halford said. 'I imagine you'd like forensic to give the place a good going-over?'

'Yes and, if you're agreeable, I'll get my scene-of-crime officer along here first thing in the morning.'

'Sure. Meanwhile, I'll have some local enquiries made about the Harrisons.' Halford frowned. 'They must have kept a low profile or we'd have heard of them. Don't like villains living in our midst without knowing it.' He paused and the frown re-formed. 'And you say Harrison was involved in an armed robbery last October?'

'That's only surmise.'

'So when he's found, the Met'll also want to talk to him.'

'That'll be up to Detective Inspector Cleave. In any event, I want first crack.'

The four officers returned to the bathroom and made an unceremonious exit the way they had entered.

'Better get this window secured, Colin,' Halford said, turn-ing to DC Cash. 'Don't want anyone else crawling in and out after we've gone.'

Intent on their own business, they paid little attention to an ice-cream van parked a short distance up the road.

It's driver, however, showed considerable covert interest in them.

He was parked in much the same place the next afternoon when Rosa and Ben made their visit. On that occasion he was surrounded by children coming home from school and had his work cut out to serve his clamorous customers and keep an eye on what was happening at number forty-two.

On both evenings he was able to phone Lee Harrison and give him an account of events. It was, after all, what he was being paid to do.

Just as Becker had conjectured, Harrison did have a second home, complete, indeed, with a second 'wife'. It was a flat in a purpose-built block not far from Epsom racecourse, where he and the lady in question passed as Mr and Mrs Joseph Allen.

Whenever trouble threatened he invariably packed his real wife off to her Belgian relatives with instructions to remain abroad until he told her to come back.

Fortunately neither of the ladies was possessive by nature (they wouldn't have lasted in his life if they had been) and knew better than to make difficulties for him. This included not asking him awkward questions. In return, he treated them both generously.

Lindy, his mistress, had had an exceptionally hard life, first as a neglected child and later when in and out of prison for stealing, and was only too glad to feel settled at last. Not asking questions was no problem to her. It was as if a kind fairy had taken her from a life of want and drudge and had installed her in unostentatious luxury.

It was from the Epsom flat that Harrison, alias Allen, phoned Keith Sidley.

'It's me, Sid,' he said. He always felt a bit self-conscious calling himself Joe to someone he'd known since his first spell in prison.

'Where've you been? I've been trying to get hold of you the last couple of days.'

137

'I've been here where I said I'd be. Sure you called the right number? Anyway, what's up?'

'You better get over here as soon as you can and I'll tell you.'

'Not to do with Les's death, is it?'

'No. Incidentally, I hope you're right about that and didn't leave any clues lying around.'

'I'm worried that the police got on to Pilatus Road so quickly. How'd they do it?'

'No good asking me! It's just as well you've checked out of that address. I take it there's no way they can trace you to the flat?'

'None. I'm sure of that.'

'Well, you'd still better be careful.'

'Did I tell you that that girl solicitor who defended Lumley had also been nosing around the bungalow?'

'No, you didn't,' Sid said flatly. 'How'd she get on to it?'

'Through the police, I imagine.'

'I don't like it. It seems to me you're at the sharp end of a murder enquiry. I don't like it at all.'

'How do you think I feel?' Harrison asked plaintively. 'Anyway, what do you want to see me about?'

'I'll tell you when you get here. It's another job for you know who. Cash in advance. But we don't want another cock-up.'

Ever since the two men had known one another, it had been accepted that Keith Sidley (Sid to his friends and enemies alike) was the senior member of the partnership. They had never aspired to join the top league of criminals, but they still made a good living. The Firley Street job, however, had gone wrong from the outset, not disastrously wrong, but annoyingly so.

It was like when major surgery isn't completely successful and further remedial action is required.

Chapter 19

Recent events had convinced Rosa that the answers to the questions posed by the Firley Street robbery lay within the walls of Bernard Hammond's shop.

It hadn't been just any old robbery of a jeweller's shop picked at random, as if from the yellow pages of the telephone directory. It had been planned as an inside job and had involved Hammond, Fingle and the two hired robbers of whom Harrison was one.

If that were right, it must have been set up as an insurance fiddle.

Supposing even that the stuff which was stolen was really worthless, so much paste, but the claim on the insurance company would still have been for over £100,000. The swap in the display cabinet could have been effected before Philip Wadingham and Susan Cunliffe arrived for work.

It was a plausible theory, though it didn't satisfactorily explain why Fingle should have been brought into the conspiracy. Perhaps he had not been such a disgruntled employee after all. He had been merely acting a part. Knowing now that he was a relative of Harrison, one could deduce that he had been paid to organise the whole thing. Harrison was clearly a professional criminal and presumably had a wide range of contacts among the criminal fraternity.

Obviously the plan required the robbery to have the appearance of being the real thing, hence the use of a gun. The fact that Bernard Hammond suffered a flesh wound would have been unintentional. The shot was probably meant to chip the wall, not injure the proprietor,

139

but Stephen Lumley's unscheduled appearance had thrown everything into confusion.

If only he had not taken to his heels and run . . .

On the other hand, the Hammonds had been quick to exploit his presence to their own advantage. He was an innocent scapegoat who had played right into their hands.

Rosa stared with a sombre expression across her office. If this were the true scenario it meant that the Hammonds had not only conspired to pervert the course of justice, but had gone further and deliberately perjured away an innocent person's liberty. It was a diabolical thing to have done and Rosa felt a surge of outrage as she pondered it.

Perjury was common enough in the courts, but in the view of most people, it was one thing for a defendant to tell lies in order to save his own skin, quite another for a witness to tell wilful lies in order to put someone else in prison.

Rosa wondered if Robin was in the office as she felt she would like to canvass her views with him. He not only was, but said he would welcome a bit of distraction.

'I'm more than ever convinced that Lumley's innocent,' she said, ensconcing herself in his visitor's chair.

'You've not wavered in that belief from the outset,' he observed. 'Though what you can do about it is a different matter. Righting injustices – if there *has* been an injustice – is a stony path to tread. Generally speaking, the powers that be just don't want to know. It upsets the public to have doubts cast on our system of justice.'

'Blow the public! What about the innocent person languishing in prison?'

'I'm afraid it happens from time to time. We all know that; or rather we suspect it, but prefer not to know. Public confidence becomes undermined if skeletons are being constantly brought out of the cupboard. Mind you, it's become a popular pastime on TV, all this investigative reporting. In my view, the presenters often spoil their case by displaying crude bias and their own vested interests. And television is the perfect medium for serving up artfully edited views, often taken out of context, under the guise of truth. Probably because they're not particularly interested in truth as such, only in a dynamic programme.' He smiled. 'Anyway, what's your particular problem?'

'My problem,' Rosa said a trifle sourly, 'is how to prove Lumley's innocence.' She then went on to give Robin her latest thoughts on the subject while he listened to her in silence.

'As I see it, your only hope is that enquiries into Fingle's murder will uncover something. Otherwise I can't see what more you can do.'

'But do you agree my theory holds together?'

'Provided one accepts that Lumley's presence at the shop was a pure coincidence.'

'Coincidences do happen, Robin,' she said with a touch of exasperation.

'I know, I know. But in criminal cases they're always greeted with suspicion. They're a bit too convenient to be accepted without question.'

'Convenient!' Rosa exploded. 'There was nothing convenient about it from Lumley's point of view and yet it's he who's protesting that it was a coincidence.'

'I think you're being a trifle naïve.'

'Just because you're a lawyer with a trained logical mind and don't like anything that can't be rationally accounted for doesn't mean that coincidences can be ignored.'

Giving her one of his more disarming smiles, he said, 'As a matter of fact, I think your theory is both ingenious and plausible, but it's still only a theory. Moreover, I don't begin to see how you'll ever prove it without outside assistance. If this man Harrison is ever caught and talks, you may find your theory proved for you. On the other hand, it's possible that what he says will prove you utterly wrong.'

'Then at least I'll be able to start all over again.'

'I think you should be prepared for him to say that Lumley was in the robbery up to his neck.'

'Because he says it won't necessarily make it true,' she

remarked in a stubborn voice. 'He can hardly make things any worse for Lumley.'

Robin remained silent. He had learnt when to save his breath and it was plain that nothing he could say was going to deflect Rosa from her chosen path, though he could not help feeling that she might as well stand outside the prison and try and knock down its walls with her bare fists. Nevertheless at the back of his mind was the niggling thought that she might be proved right. It had happened before. But he still felt that lawyers ought not to become emotionally identified with their clients' causes.

On the other hand he recognised that two of his own kind in the office would make it a much less stimulating place in which to work. His junior partner's instinct and flashes of intuition were valuable assets, particularly when allied to common sense, with which Rosa was well endowed. With this final thought he gave her an affectionate smile as she made to return to her own room.

It was her habit when going to bed to turn on her small bedside radio. She liked to catch the late night news and also the weather forecast for the next day, even if she seldom remembered it when morning came. The set was permanently tuned to a local commercial station whose newscaster managed to impart an air of immediacy to the most mundane items.

That evening he was nearing the end of a saga of dramas occurring all over the capital when in his crisp, breathless voice, he announced, 'Reports are just reaching us of a woman abducted in Highgate while taking her dog out for its bedtime stroll. Stay with us for more on our next newscast.'

Rosa got into bed and switched off the radio. But for once sleep didn't readily come and she restlessly turned from side to side. It was a warm evening and her bed soon became uncomfortably hot. After half an hour she decided there was no point in lying there in increasing frustration and that it would be better to get up and let her bed cool down while she gave herself a bland and soothing drink. Then she would smooth the sheets, plump up her pillow and start again.

It was during these final preparations for a return to bed that she switched the radio on just in time to hear the same newscaster saying, '... abducted from near her home in Highgate is Mrs Carol Hammond, wife of a West End jeweller. At the moment there is no indication as to why Mrs Hammond has been kidnapped or where she is being held. Her distraught husband has gone to the station to help police in their enquiries ... '

Chapter 20

When Rosa woke the next morning, she couldn't at first identify the reason for her sense of expectation. Then recollection came flooding back.

As soon as she had dressed, she dashed out to buy a paper. She had one delivered daily, but it was unlikely to carry more than the barest report of Carol Hammond's abduction and she needed one with up-to-the-minute local news.

She had listened to the radio while she dressed, but felt that a newspaper would provide more solid detail of what had happened. The *North London Daily* had the reputation of covering events within its area almost before they had taken place, thanks to a small energetic team of faithful reporters who prided themselves on their general ubiquity.

Mrs Gupta, who, with her husband, ran the newsagent's shop round the corner from her flat, gave her a worried look as she entered.

'I am sorry, it is a new boy,' she exclaimed before Rosa could say anything. 'Your paper is most definitely on its way.'

'I'm sure it'll be there by the time I get back,' Rosa said in a pacifying voice, 'but I've come for a copy of the *North London Daily*.'

With an expression of relief, Mrs Gupta reached for one. Its headline 'Highgate Woman Abducted' assured Rosa that her dash to the newsagent had been worthwhile. Wishing Mrs Gupta a pleasant day, she hurried back to her flat.

Settling herself in the kitchen with a cup of coffee and a slice of toast and honey, she began to read.

Around ten thirty last night Mrs Carol Hammond of 116 Thruxton Lodge, Thruxton Avenue, N6, was abducted by masked men as she walked her dog not more than 200 yards from her home. She was driven away at high speed, struggling in the back of the car. The whole drama was witnessed by Mrs Grace Girling of 34 Thruxton Avenue outside whose home it took place.

Mrs Girling, who is confined to a wheel-chair, was sitting in the front window of her home. She told our reporter, 'I saw this lady coming along the pavement with her little dog. It's a King Charles spaniel. I see them most evenings, though I don't know the lady's name. I assume they live further up the avenue. I see her so often that I've come to regard her and the dog as part of my life. She was just walking past my home when a dark saloon car suddenly pulled up and a man wearing a balaclava helmet leapt out. He seized the lady and bundled her into the back of the car despite her struggles. The car was then driven off at tremendous speed. I could see that the driver was also wearing a balaclava helmet. I didn't see what happened to the little dog. I immediately shouted to my companion and told her to phone the police. I felt very shaken. It was seeing the men wearing balaclava helmets on a warm summer's evening that really scared me.'

Cora, which is the name of the dog, ran all the way home where her arrival without her mistress alerted Mr Hammond that something had happened to his wife. He immediately went out to look for her and was in the street when the police arrived at Mrs Girling's house.

Mr Hammond, who owns a jewellery shop in Firley Street, W1, told our reporter, 'My wife used to take Cora out for a walk every evening. She insisted she was perfectly safe. She was usually out for about twenty minutes. This evening she and Cora went out just after ten thirty. It occurred to me she was staying out longer than usual, but I assumed she had met a neighbour and stopped to talk, as sometimes happened. I had begun to get worried and went to look out of the window when I saw Cora running up and down outside, trailing her lead. I immediately dashed out into the road. I saw a police car draw up outside a house further along the avenue and I ran to it. By then I was sure something awful had happened to my wife. I told the officer who I was and that my wife was missing. I was told there'd been a kidnapping and it sounded as if Carol had been the victim. I am at a total loss to know who could have done this and I ask whoever it is to return her to me quickly, safe and sound. I shan't rest until I have her home.'

We understand that Mr Hammond's shop was the target for an armed raid last October, in the course of which over £100,000 worth of jewellery was stolen and Mr Hammond was wounded by a stray shot. A man was subsequently arrested and sent to prison for six years for his part in the robbery. Police say they have no reason to believe there is any connection between the robbery and last night's kidnapping. They are asking for anyone to come forward who may have information that throws light on Mrs Hammond's dramatic abduction. So far no ransom demand has been received.

Rosa put down the paper and poured herself another cup of coffee. Last night's newscast had mentioned that a distraught Bernard Hammond had gone to the station to assist police in their enquiries. This was the accepted euphemism to denote a suspect under questioning and she wondered if it meant that in the present case. If so, there must have been something about the abduction to have aroused immediate suspicion. On the other hand, it might for once mean nothing more than it said. It was, after all, perfectly reasonable in the circumstances for Bernard Hammond to be assisting the police with all the information he possessed.

She glanced at her watch. It was only just after eight o'clock. If she left home immediately she could drive up to Highgate before going to the office. There were a number

146

of features about the abduction that intrigued her and she wanted to see for herself the lie of the ground.

With a street map on the seat beside her she found Thruxton Avenue without difficulty. It was a broad, sweeping curve, tree-lined and with large houses, most of them converted into flats, on either side. From the busy main road at one end it rose in a gentle gradient to Thruxton Lodge, a large purpose-built block of flats at the top. Number thirty-four where Mrs Girling lived was a small house sandwiched between two much larger ones. It lay about halfway along on the left.

Rosa had wondered how Mrs Girling, observant as she might be, had been able to see all the detail she had described. Admittedly there was still some daylight at ten thirty on a midsummer's evening, but would it have been enough? The answer was in the affirmative, for there was also a lamppost outside number thirty-four.

After turning the car round at the top of the road, Rosa cruised gently down, coming to a halt outside Mrs Girling's house, though on the opposite side of the road. As she stared across at what she assumed to be the scene of the abduction, she became aware of a woman sitting in a wheel-chair in the porch of the house. Her interest had been transferred from the newspaper on her lap to the girl sitting in the car, which had just drawn up on the other side of the road.

After a moment's hesitation, Rosa realised she had no choice but to go across and explain her presence.

The woman kept her under wary scrutiny as she approached. As soon as Rosa was close enough, she said, 'If you're from the press I can't talk to you. The police have told me to keep my mouth shut.' Her tone was didactic, but Rosa resisted the temptation to answer in kind.

'I'm not from the press,' she said peaceably. 'I'm a solicitor with a professional interest in last night's events.'

Mrs Girling gazed at her with fresh interest. 'My niece has recently qualified as a solicitor. She's working for a television company in Manchester. I tell her she'd do better if she moved to London. What do you think?'

Rosa felt as if she were being given a credibility test.

'It depends on where her interests lie,' she said. 'If she's eventually going into private practice, there's much to be said for working in the provinces. You can choose your favourite part of the country and look for an opening. I wish her well.'

'Thank you.' She gave her chair a sudden sharp tug to avoid the sun which was shining into her eyes. 'That's better. I always sit out here after breakfast if the weather's good. It keeps me out of the way while my companion gets on with the chores.'

Rosa had noticed the open front door behind her, through which came the busybody hum of a vacuum cleaner.

'I've read this morning's *North London Daily*,' Rosa said.

Mrs Girling pulled a face. 'The police told me I shouldn't have spoken to the young reporter who called here just after they'd left. They said I could have made things more difficult for them.'

'They're never keen on witnesses talking to the press,' Rosa remarked.

'The last thing I'd want is to make things worse for that unfortunate woman.' She gazed out across the road. 'It all happened so quickly. Just there, outside my gate. I can still scarcely realise that I actually saw what I did.'

'I noticed you said that Mrs Hammond put up a struggle.'

'Yes, she struggled fiercely, but she was bundled into the back of the car before she had a chance to do anything. The man held a gloved hand over her mouth so she couldn't even scream.'

'How much of his face could you see?'

'None of it. That is, apart from his eyes. The balaclava covered the rest.'

'Did the driver remain in the car the whole time?'

'Yes, he kept the engine running. He was also wearing a balaclava. I just couldn't believe my eyes and then it was all over. I shouted to my companion and then I called the police.'

'Did your companion witness anything herself?'

'No, she was in her bedroom watching some rubbish on television.'

'I gather you'd often seen Mrs Hammond taking her dog for an evening walk?'

'Frequently, though I never knew her name until last night. Doesn't that sound awful?'

At that moment, a thin wisp of a woman wearing a bright yellow overall appeared in the doorway behind.

'I thought I heard voices,' she said. 'Are you all right, dear?'

'Perfectly all right, thank you, Celia. This lady's a solicitor.'

'Oh!' Celia said, apparently nonplussed by the information. 'I was only wondering . . . '

'I know very well what you were wondering. She's nothing to do with the press.' A frown formed on her brow as she glanced back at Rosa. 'Whose solicitor are you exactly?'

'I'm afraid I'm not at liberty to disclose that,' Rosa said in a deprecating tone as she turned to go.

Mrs Girling nodded knowingly while Celia merely stared.

Rosa had always remembered the advice given by a cynical old lecturer at law school. It was to the effect that when giving someone a dusty answer which couldn't easily be justified, you prefaced it by saying, 'for reasons which you will readily appreciate'. It won't be often, he had added, that your bluff will be called.

As she joined the slow-moving flow of traffic into central London she pondered over what she had just learnt. She was quite certain that the robbery and the abduction were connected. But how? Almost too many theories offered themselves.

She wished she knew what the police were making of it. With Carol Hammond's abduction following hard on Fingle's murder, surely even Detective Inspector Cleave could no longer affect a lack of interest in events.

Maybe she should call him.

Chapter 21

Cleave learnt about the abduction from his morning paper. He was still absorbing what he had read when his phone rang and Detective Inspector Hedley, the officer in charge of enquiries, came on the line.

'You don't have to tell me why you're calling,' Cleave said. 'I've just read about the Hammond kidnapping in the paper.'

'Ah! I have a feeling it could be connected with your robbery case. Incidentally, I gather your file on that is still open.'

'You talk about having a feeling, but do you have any evidence that there's any connection between the two?'

'Not yet. But what's your view?'

'I don't have one. I had no reason to suspect the Hammonds were up to any funny business when I investigated the robbery. It was a straightforward case with one of the robbers arrested on the spot. Bernard Hammond sustained a bullet wound in his shoulder and there was nothing faked about that. If the bullet had gone a few inches to the right, he wouldn't be walking around today and Lumley would have been charged with murder.'

'I'm wondering if the men who got away are involved in Mrs Hammond's abduction? I gather there's also a murder in Oxford that could be linked with what's happened.'

Cleave let out a snort. 'Just because the dead man once worked for Hammond doesn't strike me as particularly significant.'

'Maybe not. On the other hand—'

'Has there been any ransom demand yet?' Cleave broke in.

'No, but it's early days. They probably hope the wait will soften up old Hammond and make him more likely to meet their demands.'

'I take it you have that aspect well covered?'

'We've put a tap on his phone and we're keeping a careful eye on his home. If the kidnappers attempt to get in touch with him, we'll be waiting.' DI Hedley paused and went on, 'I can't help wondering whether the two robbers who got away are now having a second bite at the cherry. They presumably know that Hammond's worth a fair amount and reckon he'll be ready to cough up for the safe return of his wife.' When Cleave didn't immediately reply, he added, 'How does that strike you?'

'Quite frankly, it doesn't. They did very nicely out of the robbery, so why should they risk coming back? It doesn't make sense.'

'I see,' Hedley said in a flat voice. 'So you don't think there's any connection between the three crimes?'

'Let's say, I've yet to be persuaded.'

'At the moment I haven't much to go on,' Hedley remarked. 'Two men wearing balaclavas disappear into thin air with a kidnap victim in a car whose registration number we don't know. I'd have thought somebody might have seen something suspicious as they made off, but apparently not.'

'Someone may yet come forward,' Cleave said in a reassuring voice. 'Moreover, you'll have something to work on once a ransom demand has been made.'

'I hope so. I'll keep in touch. Meanwhile thanks for your help.'

Though exactly what help he'd have been hard put to say.

Later that day, Cleave received a call from Rosa. Though he had not seen or spoken to her since Lumley's trial ended, her image remained fresh in his mind.

'Good morning, Miss Epton,' he said affably. 'Do I need to ask why you're calling me?'

'Probably not. It's about Carol Hammond's abduction.'

'I doubt whether I know any more about it than you do.'

'Possibly even less,' Rosa remarked. 'I visited the scene of the crime this morning, which is probably more than you've done.'

'It certainly is. It's not my case.'

'Nevertheless, I'd be interested to hear your views, if you're prepared to talk. For instance, do you believe the abduction and the robbery have a connection?'

Cleave let out an audible sigh. 'It's far too early to say.'

'But you agree it's a possibility?'

'Almost anything's possible in this life, Miss Epton,' he said in a long-suffering tone.

'Even my client's innocence?'

'Excluding that.'

'There was definitely something phoney about that robbery,' Rosa said firmly. 'Don't you regard it as odd that you've never received any sort of tip-off as to the other men involved?'

'Not specially. All too often criminals get away without leaving any trace behind. Sometimes it's years before we pick up a clue; sometimes we never do. But I assure you that my file on the robbery remains open.'

Soothing words, Rosa reflected with a touch of scorn. Aloud she said, 'It's clear to me that this man Harrison who's wanted for questioning in connection with Fingle's murder was one of the two robbers. Do you agree?'

'He may have been, but there's no evidence of it.'

'And if he is, it strengthens the connection between all three crimes.'

'Possibly, but I don't see it helping Lumley.'

Rosa realised there was no point in raking over this particular issue which was one of total contention between them.

'Have you had a further look into the insurance fiddle angle?' she enquired.

'Between ourselves, old Hammond's insurance company is still stalling over his claim. Not that insurance companies ever pay up with the alacrity they'd have us believe.'

'Are they withholding payment because they think there was something fishy about the robbery?'

'They didn't like the fact that the alarm system had chosen that moment to go on the blink.'

'As I recall, it had been on the blink the week previous to the robbery.'

'That's right. It had been attended to, but then went kaput again.'

'Are you suggesting it had been tampered with?'

'No. The evidence as to that didn't help one way or the other. But it's been enough to make the insurance company stall. I may say we found no evidence that Bernard Hammond was in any sort of financial difficulty. On the contrary, he's an extremely wealthy man and doesn't have a creditor in sight. We looked into that aspect as part of our general enquiries.' Cleave paused. 'Moreover, there was nothing phoney about the bullet that went through his shoulder. That was genuine lead penetrating genuine flesh.' After a further pause he added, 'I still believe that Lumley could tell us all a great deal more if he chose. Maybe he'll yet do so.'

Chapter 22

The Pearce boys, Guy aged thirteen and Rob younger by two years, had been looking forward to the picnic all the week and praying that the weather would remain fine.

Their family outings to Epping Forest were always memorable occasions. What made them especially enjoyable was their parents' well-judged participation in the boys' activities, not to mention their mother's skill in filling the hamper with all their favourite things.

Picnics in the forest were special treat occasions reserved for birthdays and other events that called for a bit of extra celebration.

They always made for exactly the same spot which they had come to regard as their own. It involved quite a walk from where they parked the car, but was well worth the effort. They viewed with contempt those who squatted beside their cars at the roadside breathing in lungfuls of polluted air as they ate.

'The forecast's good for tomorrow,' Jim Pearce announced after listening to the weather news that Saturday evening.

And, indeed, when it came, Sunday showed itself to be a perfect day. They reached the area around noon and twenty minutes later arrived at their own clearing, which seemed to be waiting for them, as if specially reserved.

'One day we'll find someone else has got here first,' Jim Pearce observed to his wife as he put down the picnic hamper.

'God forbid!' Mrs Pearce said feelingly as she observed the expressions on her sons' faces. To behold so much contentment and joyous anticipation was, she felt, ample reward for having to cope with the rougher patches of domestic life.

'How long before we eat?' Guy enquired.

'Half an hour.'

'OK if we go and explore?'

'Yes,' his father said, 'but don't go too far. Stay within shouting distance.'

'Why don't you come with us, Dad?' Rob said.

'I will after lunch. Now, off you go, but not too far.'

'Don't worry,' Guy said as he and his brother bounded away.

'I suppose it's all right to let them go off on their own,' Mrs Pearce said in a resigned voice. 'Though I confess I get more worried every time we come. One reads of so many awful things happening to children these days.'

'We can't keep them wrapped in cotton wool,' her husband observed. 'Anyway, Guy's pretty sensible and wouldn't lead Rob into trouble.'

'What about the other way round?'

Jim Pearce laughed good-naturedly. 'No way. We're lucky in having two sons who get on so well together. I suppose that one day they'll grow apart, but I like to think of them remaining good friends whatever the future holds.'

'You really are wearing your rose-tinted spectacles today.'

'Why not? It's a glorious day and I'm out with my favourite wife and kids.'

In the distance they could hear the boys shouting to each other. Mrs Pearce gave a sudden shiver.

'What's up, love? You're not still worrying about them, are you?'

'I suppose I am. Nasty things can happen so suddenly. Children disappear in broad daylight and turn up later as murder victims.'

'If it worries you that much, we'd better not come again,' her husband said with a sigh. 'Though I'm not sure how we'll explain it to the boys.' He moved over to where his wife was kneeling as she unpacked the hamper and put an arm round

155

her shoulder. 'As soon as you're ready, I'll give them a shout. The summons to food is one they always answer.'

'It's been reading about that poor paper-boy who vanished on his delivery round and was found sadistically murdered. He was almost exactly Guy's age. If anything like that should ever happen to Guy or Rob . . . . '

'Now you're being really morbid, darling. They're much more likely to be knocked down by a car when they're crossing the road than be kidnapped.'

'I don't find that terribly comforting,' she said.

'All I'm saying is that you can't protect them against every conceivable peril. One can only teach them to react sensibly to each situation and, on the whole, I reckon we've been reasonably successful.' He cocked an ear. 'Anyway, it's either a stampede of elephants or them returning now.'

A second or two later, Guy, closely followed by Rob, came crashing through the undergrowth. They stood wild-eyed and panting while their parents stared at them aghast.

'What's happened?' their father asked, aware of a constriction of his throat.

'We've found a dead woman,' Guy gasped.

'I saw her first,' Rob said, not without a note of pride.

'A dead woman? Where?'

'Over there,' they chorused, pointing vaguely into the bushes.

'She's probably just sleeping,' their father said trying to sound practical.

'No, she's definitely dead. You've got to come, Dad.'

Jim Pearce turned to his younger son. 'You stay here with Mummy, while I go back with Guy.' His tone carried a firm note of paternal authority.

Following his son through the surround of bushes and along an overgrown path, they reached a bracken-covered area where the trees were more spread out and one could hear the hum of traffic on one of the busy roads that intersected the forest.

'There!' Guy suddenly exclaimed, pointing a few yards ahead of him and dropping back behind his father.

Nothing had equipped Jim Pearce for dealing with dead bodies discovered on a family picnic, but he was a practical man; moreover, he was conscious of being under the close scrutiny of his thirteen-year-old son. It was not a time to show timidity.

He stepped cautiously forward until he was more or less looking straight down at the body. It was that of a blonde woman, lying on her back with arms and legs flung wide. He observed that both bore scratch marks and that her face was streaked with dirt. But, that apart, he was unable to detect any sign of injury. There was no obvious cause of death. It could be that she had succumbed to an overdose of drugs. He was deciding what he ought to do when the woman suddenly opened her eyes and blinked, at the same time letting out a low moan.

'Please help me,' she said in a hoarse whisper.

Kneeling down beside her, Jim Pearce put an arm beneath her head and gently brought her into a sitting position.

'Are you badly hurt?' he asked, noticing for the first time red weals around her wrists.

'I think I must have fainted,' she said weakly. 'I managed to get out of the van when they stopped and I just ran and ran until I dropped.' Then, as if she felt further explanation was required, she added, 'They were moving me to a new hide-out.'

Jim Pearce frowned as he sought to make sense out of what she was saying.

'Are you the lady that was kidnapped the other day?' Guy asked in an eager voice. 'It was in all the papers.'

'They wouldn't let me see any papers,' she said. 'But my name's Carol Hammond. I was abducted near my home last . . . ' She paused. 'What day is it today?'

'Sunday,' Guy informed her.

'Let me help you to your feet,' Jim Pearce said. 'I must let my wife know what's happened, then I'll drive you to the nearest police station.'

'Where did the men hold you? And how many of them were there?' Guy asked keenly.

'Stop asking questions,' his father said sharply. 'Run ahead and tell Mummy what's happened.'

Though it was apparent that the picnic would have to be abandoned, the boys were not disposed to make any fuss about the dramatic change of plan. As they piled into the back of the car with their mother, Guy was busy rehearsing in his mind the story he would tell his friends, while Rob, equally silent, saw himself facing the nation's television cameras and possibly being presented with a medal.

Jim Pearce was about to start the car when he turned to Carol who was sitting next to him.

'I know I said I'd drive you to the nearest police station, but perhaps you'd sooner go straight home. I'm quite prepared to drive you there.'

She shook her head. 'No, a police station will be better.'

'If we see a public call-box on the way, you may like to phone home and say you're all right?'

Her response to the suggestion was immediate and negative. 'No. Please just take me to a police station.' Then as if aware that she sounded ungracious, she added, 'You've been so kind. I don't know what would have happened if you hadn't found me.' She turned her head and smiled at the boys. 'I'm afraid I've ruined your picnic.'

'That's all right,' Guy said generously. 'It's been worth it.'

During the time she had been in their company she had said very little about herself save that she lived in Highgate. She was wearing a wedding ring, but made no mention of a husband. Mrs Pearce assumed that she was still in a state of shock, which was natural enough. She had accepted the offer of coffee at the picnic site, but had declined alcohol-free beer and Coca Cola.

It took them fifteen minutes' driving to find a police station. As he pulled up outside, Jim Pearce said, 'I'll come in with you. The police will probably want to have my name and address and they can get in touch with me later.' To his wife he added, 'You stay here with the boys. I shan't be long.'

Twenty minutes later he emerged from the station and got back into the car.

'We could go back to the forest and have our picnic after all,' he said. 'It's not too late.'

But the mood seemed to have passed and the boys were obviously eager to get home and relate their adventure to their friends.

'Funny sort of woman,' Jim Pearce remarked to his wife later that afternoon when they were alone. 'I'd have expected a few hysterics, but there were none.'

'They may come later. Though she seemed composed, I had the impression that she was completely uptight. Frightened, even.'

'I suppose that's not surprising after what she's been through.'

'Maybe not,' his wife remarked doubtfully. Then in a musing tone she added, 'It'll be interesting to follow developments.'

Chapter 23

Two days later Detective Inspectors Cleave and Hedley, together with Detective Chief Inspector Becker, met in a room at Scotland Yard under the chairmanship of Detective Chief Superintendent Kershaw. Their brief was to pool information and co-ordinate their enquiries in the light of information supplied by Carol Hammond.

'I hope we've now agreed that the Firley Street robbery, Fingle's murder and Mrs Hammond's abduction are almost certainly connected,' Kershaw said firmly.

Becker and Hedley nodded while Cleave continued to look sceptical.

'If we're right in thinking that Hammond's hand lies behind all three crimes, that doesn't necessarily put Lumley in the clear,' Kershaw went on, addressing his remark to Cleave. 'He would still have been one of the conspirators, even if the nature of the conspiracy is different. In fact, to my innocent mind, he's the most obvious conspirator of all. Hammond would have approached him to take part because he knew how vulnerable his financial difficulties made him. Once Hammond decided to stage a fake robbery, I imagine Lumley was one of the first people he approached. He doubtless applied the same sort of pressure to Fingle who was vulnerable for the same reason. I'm sure he'd have needed no second invitation to take part. Almost certainly it was Fingle who brought in the other two, Harrison who was a relative and the man named Sid whom we've yet to identify.' He glanced round the table, his eyes coming to rest on DI Hedley. 'From what Mrs Hammond told you, it's clear that it came as a total shock to her to discover her husband's complicity.'

'Yes, sir, particularly that he was behind her abduction. That really shook her. Although her captors kept her wrists and legs tied and she was also blindfolded, she was still able to hear. She described in graphic detail how she was lying on this camp-bed and the two men were in the adjoining room with the connecting door ajar. She's quite definite that one of the men said, "Hammond's going to phone this evening with further instructions." The other commented that he wished he'd make up his mind quickly what they were to do with her as he hadn't bargained on becoming a jailer. That was the day before they moved her and she was able to escape from the back of the van and found herself in Epping Forest, even though she had no idea where she was until Mr Pearce and his son discovered her.'

'Very convenient for her that the van stopped when it did,' Cleave remarked sardonically.

Hedley gave a shrug. 'She says the engine had been playing up for several miles and the driver had been cursing it. She's not a motor mechanic and can only say it wasn't accelerating properly. Eventually they stopped and both the men got out.' Hedley paused and gave Cleave a hard look. 'I naturally questioned her closely about her escape. On the face of it, I agree, it had an element of "with one bound, Jack was free". However, she told me how she'd persuaded them to loosen her bonds for the journey as her wrists and ankles had become badly chafed. Moreover, because she couldn't see out of the van, they'd removed her blindfold. When they stopped to look at the engine one of them came round to the back to fetch some tools and didn't bother to re-lock the rear door. They were both so occupied with their heads under the car bonnet that she was able to get out and disappear into the bushes before they knew what had happened.'

'Satisfied?' Kershaw said, looking at Cleave.

'It still sounds a bit glib to me, sir.'

'So what's *your* theory?' Kershaw asked, with a touch of asperity.

Cleave bit his lip. 'I've not had the opportunity of inter-viewing her, sir. I'd like to test her story a bit more before accepting it. I'm not criticising Inspector Hedley,' he added quickly, 'but I still can't see why she should have been abducted in the first place.'

'Mrs Hammond's positive that her husband planned to have her killed. First there would have been a ransom demand and when this wasn't met, she'd have been murdered on her husband's orders. She says their marriage was washed up and he wanted her out of his life. Having her killed, she suggests, would have been cheaper than an expensive divorce settle-ment.' Hedley paused and went on, 'It's my belief that there were a number of factors at play, one of them being Fingle's death. That may have become unavoidable, but it opened up a can of worms.'

Becker leaned forward and spoke for the first time. 'As I see it, Fingle had been part of the robbery plot, but then fell out with the others and became a danger. His meetings with Miss Epton and the half-written letter to her prove that he was about to spill the beans. That was why he had to be silenced.'

'What precise form would those beans have taken, I won-der?' Kershaw enquired, looking round the table.

'A readiness to grass on the others.'

'Which others?'

'Harrison for sure, and Sid, whoever he may be.'

'I'm convinced Lumley could throw light on the whole affair if he was minded to talk,' Cleave said.

'Lumley can't have had anything to do with Fingle's murder or Mrs Hammond's abduction,' Kershaw observed.

'Maybe not, sir, but he could still tell us why they took place.'

'At least you now seem to agree that all three crimes are connected,' Kershaw remarked.

Cleave looked annoyed. 'I've never ruled it out,' he said stiffly. 'It's just that I wasn't persuaded. I still have some doubts.'

Chief Superintendent Kershaw sighed. He had the im-pression that beneath the urbanity, there were a number of irresistible forces meeting immovable objects. He turned to DI Hedley.

'I reckon you should concentrate your efforts on Hammond. The fact that he denies having anything to do with his wife's abduction isn't sufficient reason to stop hammering him. To suggest, as you say he does, that she must have been either drugged or hypnotised to accuse him of arranging her abduction verges on the absurd. Particularly as the doctor who examined her after her escape found nothing wrong apart from a few bruises and lacerations and certainly nothing amiss with her mental state.'

Hedley pursed his lips. 'Hammond's made it quite clear that if we seek to question him further, he'll insist on having his solicitor present.'

'That in itself could be construed as an admission of guilt,' Becker remarked. 'Not in a court of law, of course, but as a common-sense deduction. After all, one would expect him, in the circumstances, to co-operate fully with the police, unless he's got something to hide.'

'Where's Mrs Hammond at the moment?' Kershaw asked DI Hedley.

'She's staying with a divorced sister in Croydon.'

'Does her husband know she's there?'

'I don't know, but he could find out easily enough.'

'Meanwhile he's still at the flat in Highgate?'

'Yes.'

'Have they been in touch at all since she regained her freedom?'

'I can't say, sir. He may have tried to contact her, but she had no intention of seeing or speaking to him.'

'Is she scared he'll try and harm her?'

'I think she reckons he wouldn't dare so soon after his last scheme failed. Nevertheless, we're keeping an unobtrusive eye on her sister's house.'

Chief Inspector Kershaw puffed out his cheeks and drew a deep breath.

'Hmm! Well, I propose we step up our search for Harrison and the man called Sid and at the same time find a bit of leverage to use on Bernard Hammond. There must be something.' He gave each of them a look that was a mixture of royal wish and exhortation. 'Three connected crimes should give us three times as many leads to unearthing the truth.'

Whatever his audience of three thought of this proposition, it elicited no comment.

Chapter 24

Rosa's mind remained obsessed with how she was to prove Stephen Lumley's innocence. As each fresh development failed to provide her with more than temporary momentum, she became increasingly frustrated.

She had hoped that Les Fingle's murder would lead to a quick arrest and an uncovering of the truth. Instead, the investigation seemed to have run into the ground with Harrison's disappearance. There followed Carol Hammond's abduction which had left her puzzled and without a clear thought as to what lay behind it. She felt she was running out of ideas and yet instinct told her that the truth of what had happened in Firley Street that October morning was almost within her grasp.

She knew that if she were unable to satisfy the authorities that her client was the object of a grievous miscarriage of justice, the outlook for Lumley was bleak indeed. It could be twelve months before an appeal was heard, always assuming he was granted leave to appeal which was by no means certain. An appeal against sentence might result in a reduction of the six years he was serving, but an appeal against conviction was a forlorn hope unless compelling evidence turned up which had not been available at the trial and which the appeal court could not overlook. Without such evidence, Lumley had no hope at all, for the usual grounds of appeal, namely a serious misdirection by the trial judge or a verdict which went against the weight of the evidence so as to be perverse, were simply not available. Judge Grapham had not put a foot wrong, or certainly not sufficiently wrong to give the appeal court cause to worry.

It was while she was in this state of considerable frustration that she heard about Carol Hammond's escape from her captors. She spent some time trying to decide which of her various theories best accommodated this latest turn of events.

She had been inclined to think that the two Hammonds had been co-conspirators in the original robbery and that the abduction had been a put-up job, even though she was unable to perceive any sense in it. But now Carol Hammond was free again and apparently making serious allegations against her husband, something she, Rosa, had learnt from a newspaper reporter.

All her theories revolved round a web of machinations on the part of husband and wife and she felt she must be able to deduce something from this latest development. Something that cool, analytical thought would put into a proper context . . .

Ten minutes later she got up from her desk and hurried out of her office.

'If anyone wants me, Steph, I'll be out for about an hour,' she said as she passed through the entrance lobby over which Stephanie kept a magisterial eye.

It was early afternoon and she told the taxi driver to put her down at the end of Firley Street. She decided as a first step to walk past the shop and glance in to see who was behind the counter. She recalled Susan Cunliffe having told her that Bernard Hammond rarely left the shop at lunch-time unless he had an engagement, but was wont to slip out for a breath of air and a cup of coffee around three o'clock. With luck, therefore, he would be out now. As for his wife, Rosa couldn't imagine that she had returned to work.

She had just drawn level with the shop when a black blind with the word 'closed' printed on it in silver was pulled down over the glass panel of the door. With a frustrated sigh she walked on a couple of yards and paused in front of the adjoining shop.

She reasoned that somebody would shortly emerge. Of course it was possible that the blind had been drawn by Bernard Hammond himself, who was not, in fact, preparing to leave, but proposing to work undisturbed in the rear office. Presumably he would do that only if he wanted total privacy. But privacy to do what, Rosa wondered? All she could think of was to make phone calls without being overheard.

She was considering this and other possibilities when the door opened and Philip Wadingham and Susan Cunliffe came out. After a few words together on the pavement, Wadingham walked off in the other direction, while Susan turned and immediately caught sight of Rosa. She was clearly taken completely by surprise and didn't appear sure how to react to Rosa's friendly smile.

'Can we go somewhere and talk?' Rosa said urgently. Observing Susan's uncertain expression she added, 'I didn't let you down last time you agreed to talk to me, did I? And I give you the same promise if you'll talk to me now. It really is terribly important. I feel you have your own doubts about Stephen Lumley's guilt and I'm sure you don't want to think of him rotting in prison for years to come.'

'You're still fighting to prove his innocence?'

'Very much so; particularly as a lot of things have happened since the trial that must have left you as dazed as I am.'

'Where do you want to talk?'

'Wherever you suggest.'

'There's a café two streets along on the left. It'll be fairly empty now and I'm not known there.' She gave Rosa a faint smile. 'I'm a bit on edge these days.'

'That's hardly surprising. Incidentally, is the shop closed for the day?'

'Mr Hammond's there. He said he had work to do in the office and didn't want to have any interruptions. He told Philip and me we could go home.'

'Any idea what work he was referring to?'

'I imagine he's making phone calls.'

'In view of what's happened, aren't the police likely to have put a tap on the line?'

167

'There's a second unlisted number. It's one of those cordless phones which Mr Hammond keeps in a drawer of his desk. Philip and I are not supposed to know about it.'

In Rosa's experience, people with secret phones usually had something they didn't want the world to know about.

As Susan had surmised the café was virtually empty. Indeed its only customers were a young couple holding hands across a table and gazing into each other's eyes with expressions of intense yearning. The café's proprietor gave his new arrivals a dazzling smile over the top of a vast coffee machine that had the dimensions of a one-time cinema organ.

Rosa ordered two cups of cappuccino and carried them over to the corner table where Susan was sitting. Meanwhile the young couple remained in silent, but seemingly potent communication.

'I imagine life in the shop has been fairly uncomfortable these past few days,' Rosa remarked by way of opening what she hoped would be a rewarding dialogue.

'It's been absolutely awful,' Susan said with feeling. 'If I'd not felt that I owed a certain loyalty to Mr Hammond, I'd have left.'

'What was his reaction to his wife's abduction?'

'He didn't come into the shop the following day. I gather he spent most of the time with the police. But when he came in the day after that he looked totally exhausted. He said very little about what had happened and told us nothing that Philip and I hadn't already read in the papers. He shut himself away in the office and said he didn't wish to deal with any customers. Then came the weekend with Mrs Hammond turning up in Epping Forest and when he came in on Monday morning he was even less inclined to talk.' She paused. 'Though I did notice that he spent a large part of the day on the phone. I can't tell you whom he talked to as the door remained firmly closed the whole time.'

'I thought it was only a curtained doorway between the shop and the office,' Rosa said with a slight frown.

'There's a sliding door as well which is normally kept open and only closed when he wants complete privacy.'

'I'd be very interested to hear your theory about Mrs Hammond's abduction.'

Susan stirred her coffee as though it were a task requiring great care.

'I feel it has to be something to do with the robbery,' she said at last.

This was scarcely a revelation and Rosa went on, 'In what way do you think there's a connection?'

'Nothing's been the same since the robbery. At first, I imagined it was due to the shock of what had happened, but then I began to realise there was more to it. Mr and Mrs Hammond had changed. They were different people. Though they remained the same on the surface, I could detect tensions. It wasn't that they quarrelled or shouted at each other and yet they'd altered.'

'Did they seem particularly relieved by the outcome of the trial?'

'Not exactly relieved. They didn't gloat or rejoice over Stephen Lumley being sent to prison. Carol Hammond said several times how she wished the other two men had been caught.'

'What was their reaction to Fingle's murder?'

'I never heard them refer to it.' She gave Rosa a quizzical look. 'Do you believe it was connected with the robbery?'

Rosa nodded. 'I'm convinced that it was.'

'But that makes everything even worse. I mean, murder . . . '

'You still haven't told me your theory about Mrs Hammond's abduction,' Rosa said in a coaxing tone.

For a while Susan remained silent. Then in a deeply reflective tone she said, 'Things don't look good for Mr Hammond, do they?'

Before Rosa could follow up the observation, Susan Cunliffe got up hastily from the table.

'I didn't realise it was so late,' she said, glancing at her watch. Then with a slightly apologetic smile she added, 'I'm sorry, but I really don't want to talk any more. It's not that I have anything to hold back, but I'm utterly confused by everything that's happened.' She met Rosa's eyes. 'And scared.'

After the abrupt departure of her companion, Rosa sat in silent thought as she slowly finished her coffee. She supposed she had somehow forced Susan to look at things she preferred not to see. Ten minutes later, she got up from the table and made for the door. The proprietor was leaning on the counter reading a paper and gave Rosa another gleaming smile. The young couple were still locked in silent communication.

She walked back into Firley Street and turned in the direction of Hammond's jewellery shop. Conscious that she was playing truant from the office she was determined not to return empty-handed. She reached the shop and pressed the bell at the side of the still-shuttered door. She could hear it ring somewhere inside, but nobody came. She gave it a further vigorous push, but there was still no reply.

It was of course possible that Bernard Hammond had locked up and departed while she and Susan Cunliffe had been at the café. But she felt that he was still inside.

Aware that an old man had stopped on the pavement and was watching her with dispassionate interest, she gave the bell another prolonged ring.

Suddenly the blind was pulled aside and Bernard Hammond peered out. He shook his head crossly and pointed at the 'closed' sign. As he did so he gave Rosa a further glance and a look of slow recognition came into his eyes.

It was a further two minutes before he had switched off the burglar alarm, turned several keys in locks and pulled back a number of bolts. When he eventually opened the door it was with anything but a welcoming smile.

'What do you want?' he asked coldly.

'I think you know who I am?'

'You were my nephew's solicitor.'

'I need to talk to you.'

170

'Why should I want to talk to *you*?'

'It's my belief, Mr Hammond, that you're in deep trouble. You could find that talking to me will help you.'

After a second's frowning hesitation, he opened the door just wide enough and Rosa stepped inside.

Chapter 25

It had been a good day. The sun hadn't stopped shining and he had picked four winners out of six, which meant that he would be going home with over £300 more than he had arrived with. He felt relaxed for the first time in weeks, assisted by a plentiful intake of beer. Usually he drank to drown his sorrows, but today it had been to enhance his pleasure.

He reckoned he would stop and have a few more drinks on his way home and then he would take Lindy out to a slap-up dinner. There was nothing like a successful day's racing to cheer one up.

As he manoeuvred out of the car park, he had a sharp altercation with the driver of a car that pushed its way into the queue immediately ahead of him. Just before they reached the junction with the main road where a young constable was on traffic duty, he took the opportunity of evening the score. The car ahead stopped suddenly and he rammed it. Nothing serious, but sufficient to dent its shining paintwork. As the driver jumped out with a furious expression, he pulled quickly out of line and overtook him. He reached the main road and was about to make a left turn before accelerating happily away. 'Serve the bugger right,' he murmured to himself. 'He shouldn't have tried to cut me up in the first place.'

He was aware that the other driver was now shouting for all the world to hear and saw the young Constable beckon to him to stop.

'Did you run into the back of that car, sir?' the Constable asked.

'I don't think so.'

'He seems to think you did.'

'Too bad! Anyway, I'm in a bit of a hurry.'

'Just pull into the side, will you, sir.'

'Look, I'm in a hurry.'

'Been drinking too, sir, have you?' the Constable asked, sniffing the air inside the car. 'I'd like to see your licence and certificate of insurance.'

'I haven't got them with me.'

'What's your name?'

'Harri . . . Joseph Allen.'

'Harry Joseph Allen?'

'No, just Joseph Allen.'

'Why did you say Harry then?'

'He's a mate of mine. I'd been thinking of him when you stopped me.'

'Where do you live, Mr Allen?'

'Epsom.'

He no longer knew or cared whether the sun was still shining for a smouldering fury possessed his mind. To add to his sense of affront, the Constable in question didn't even look old enough to have started shaving. He had a smooth, rosy complexion which completely belied his authoritative manner.

While Lee Harrison sat fuming, the Constable spoke on his radio.

'There's a patrol car on its way, sir, and as soon as it arrives, I'll be asking you to take a breath test.'

'Look, officer, I really am in a hurry.'

'So you keep on saying, sir.'

'My wife's ill.'

'That why you came to the races?'

Harrison reached into his trouser pocket and fetched out a £20 note.

'Take this and let's call it a day.'

The Constable gave him a contemptuous look. 'That's bribery, sir,' he said, taking the note and initialling it, after recording the time and date at one corner.

By the time the patrol car had arrived and a breath test had confirmed that he was well over the legal limit, Harrison had sunk into a sullen silence. He was not so drunk that he was unable to appreciate the full extent of his predicament. It was too late for post-mortems, the future was now all that mattered. How much did the police know? Of course, once they took his fingerprints, he would need a whole range of quick answers. But for the time being he would stay silent and say nothing. In a situation as precarious as his, it was much easier to talk yourself into trouble than out of it.

It was only as he was about to be driven to the police station that he realised the driver of the car he had rammed had melted away in the ensuing confusion. He hoped he would have a fatal accident on his way home.

As he sat squashed in the rear seat of the patrol car, he overheard the young Constable murmur to his Sergeant, 'There's something dodgy about his name, too. I don't believe it's Allen at all.'

Well, they need not think he was going to help them put a noose round his neck. Somehow he must con them into giving him police bail. Without it, he had no way of letting Sid know what had happened.

At the thought of Sid's reaction he gave a small shiver, so that the officer sitting next to him threw him a wary glance.

Despite being an out-and-out villain, Sid was something of a puritan. He had never approved of Lee's visits to the races. Moreover, Sid's displeasure wasn't something to be lightly incurred. And just when the Hammond affair looked like paying a further dividend.

He shivered again, this time accompanied by a muted groan.

Chapter 26

Rosa walked away from the shop in Firley Street at about the same time as Lee Harrison's third winner was romping home, though her mood was very different from his at that particular moment.

She was hot and angry and aware that she had come off second-best in her battle of wits with Bernard Hammond. It was all too clear that he had allowed her into the shop simply to find out what she knew. Once he discovered that theory and speculation were her only tools, he had called her bluff.

He had vigorously rejected any suggestion of complicity in the robbery and had gone so far as to threaten to sue her for defamation if she spread it abroad that he had instigated his wife's abduction. He insisted, moreover, that every word he had spoken in the witness-box at Lumley's trial had been the truth.

Rosa had tried every tactic she could think of to break through his defences, but without avail. His righteous indignation increased with every insinuating question she asked.

'Mr Snaith was asking where you were,' Stephanie said when Rosa walked back into the office. 'I think he'd like a word with you.'

Rosa received the information with a dour nod. She didn't feel in the mood to talk to anyone, but supposed she had better find out what Robin wanted.

'Stephanie says you want to see me,' she said as she entered her partner's room.

He looked up with an expression of mild surprise. 'Nothing

special,' he said. 'When I got back I asked if you were in, but Stephanie said you'd gone out in something of a hurry. She must have assumed I wanted to talk to you about something in particular.'

'I've just paid a visit to Hammond's shop in Firley Street,' Rosa said in a flat voice.

'A profitable visit?' he enquired, though her expression told him the question was unnecessary.

'Anything but. In fact, I made a fool of myself,' she said, and went on to tell him what had happened.

'Rather like when you try and cross-examine a witness without proper ammunition. You don't make much of an impression.'

'I hoped I'd be able to scare him into making an admission of some sort.'

'He's a tougher nut than you gave him credit for,' Robin observed. 'Though that's not altogether surprising. After all, he would have needed a strong nerve to have got up to all the chicanery you suspect him of. A bogus robbery and all that.' In a quietly reflective tone, he went on, 'I still can't see why he should have arranged to be shot in the shoulder. That seems to me to be going further than realism required.'

'The bullet was probably intended to miss him, but in the general confusion, he got in its path.' Rosa paused and frowned. 'I wonder . . . ' she began, then fell silent with a thoughtful expression.

'Did he offer any explanation as to why his wife hadn't returned to him?'

'He told me quite bluntly to mind my own business. I might have done better if I'd begun by asking him that. As it was, by the time I got round to it, he realised I was on a fishing expedition and was determined not to talk.'

'He'd called your bluff?'

'Exactly.'

'And yet the fact that he let you into the shop at all is significant. He wouldn't have done that, I feel, unless he was anxious to discover just what you'd found out about him.'

'That's a point,' Rosa observed.

176

'It could indicate that he doesn't have such a clear conscience as he'd like the world to believe.'

'So what can I do now, Robin?' she asked in a despairing voice.

'Nothing, until there's a further development.'

'Meanwhile Stephen Lumley languishes in prison ticking off the days of his sentence on a calendar.'

Unable to think of a helpful reply, Robin remained silent.

Rosa returned home that evening tired and dispirited. She had not been back more than half an hour when her phone rang. She glared at it as she reluctantly moved to lift the receiver.

'Rosa, it's me, Peter,' exclaimed an ebullient Peter Chen.

'Where are you, Peter?' she asked excitedly.

'Hong Kong.' He sounded surprised by the question.

'Oh! You sound as if you're in the next room. I hoped you might be calling from Heathrow.'

'I'll definitely be back in a couple of weeks.'

'I can't wait to see you.'

'And I can't wait to make love to you again.'

Rosa giggled. Having been brought up in a country parsonage, such uninhibited declarations of intent on the telephone embarrassed her, even after a decade of involvement in the seamier side of the law.

Nevertheless, Peter's call acted like a tonic and she went to bed feeling more cheerful than she had all day. As she began to undress she switched on her bedside radio in time to catch an item about a man who had been detained as he was leaving some racecourse. Detectives from Oxford, said the newscaster, were on their way to interview him in connection with the murder in that city of one Leslie Fingle.

Though she had missed hearing the detainee's name, she was certain it must be Lee Harrison, in which case there was a real breakthrough at last.

Earlier that evening, Keith Sidley had phoned Lindy Perkins, alias Mrs Joseph Allen.

'Joe there?' he asked in his usual brusque manner, remembering to give his partner in crime his going name.

'No, he's not back yet, Sid.'

'Where's he gone to?'

'He went to the races. I was expecting him back by seven. He said he'd be home by then.'

'It's now nine.'

'I know. I can't think what's happened to him.'

'Get him to call me as soon as he comes in,' Sid said and rang off.

Lindy replaced the receiver and put out her tongue at it. She had never liked Sid, though there was nothing she could do about it. She was always polite to him for Joe's sake, but she wished she didn't have to be.

It was around two o'clock the following morning that she was awakened from a fitful sleep by a prolonged ringing of the doorbell. She assumed it must be Joe and that he had managed to mislay his key. She hurried to open the door and found herself confronted by two strange men and a woman.

'Police,' said one of the men, as the three of them thrust their way into the flat.

An identical scene was being enacted some seven miles away where Sid lived, except in that case it was three armed officers who burst in on him.

Not all his girlfriend's entreaties, curses and hysterics deflected them from making a thorough search of the place before removing Sid to a nearby police station.

Chapter 27

Two days later Detective Chief Superintendent Kershaw called another meeting of the three investigating officers. It was at once apparent that Chief Inspector Becker was the happiest of those present. Lee Harrison had been charged with Fingle's murder and Becker was confident of a conviction.

When informed that his thumbprint had been found on a roll of Polo mints in the car which had been Fingle's tomb for several days, he was stunned into total silence for a while. There followed a number of unconvincing explanations as to how it might have got there. Becker noted these before telling him that cord, identical with that used to strangle Fingle, had been found in the garage of his home in Pilatus Road. Eventually he had admitted being responsible for Fingle's death, but asserted it had been in self-defence after Fingle had launched an attack on him. At this Becker had told him with some satisfaction that the medical evidence showed that the dead man had been strangled from behind.

It had been an interrogation at which Becker held all the trumps and he had played them with skill and cunning. He had informed Harrison of Sidley's own detention and had insinuated that he, Harrison, looked like becoming the fall guy. When it became a question of whose skin to save, Lee Harrison was never in any doubt that his own took priority.

Becker put it to him that Fingle had been killed because he was about to tell the truth about the robbery. The discovery of two of the items of stolen jewellery in Sid's flat, or more precisely in the possession of Sid's girlfriend, had proved a most useful piece of leverage. Cursing Sid for his stupidity, he simply said that Fingle had organised the whole thing and that was all he knew. He also seized the opportunity of declaring that he had no prior knowledge of Sid carrying a loaded firearm and would have expressed his disapproval if he had known.

As to Carol Hammond's abduction, he denied having any part in it.

'What it amounts to,' Kershaw observed, 'is that he admits, even if equivocally, what he knows we can prove and denies the rest.'

Becker couldn't care less about the abduction, but could scarcely say so.

Turning to Cleave, Kershaw went on, 'I don't suppose it'll take the matter any further, but I take it you'll be putting Harrison and Sidley up for identification to see if either of the Hammonds or the two shop assistants can pick them out.'

'Seeing that they were well disguised that's unlikely.'

'I realise that, but . . . '

'And, anyway, if Harrison admits taking part in the robbery, is an identification parade necessary?'

'Hmm! Well, it's not something we need decide now. But don't forget that Sidley denies participation.'

'The diamond ring and clasp his girlfriend had in her possession are pretty good evidence.'

'He's explained that by saying he got them off Harrison.'

'Nobody's going to believe that. And there's the revolver that was found at his flat. If ballistic evidence can show that the bullet recovered from Hammond's shoulder was fired from that revolver, we've got Sidley by his balls.'

'He'll probably say that Harrison asked him to look after the revolver for him, which, as a friend, he was only too happy to do,' Becker said with a smile.

'What's clear,' Kershaw remarked, 'is that they're shaping up for a nice cut-throat defence. We've got them both remanded in custody, though Sidley's only on a holding charge in relation to his possession of stolen jewellery and his unlawful possession of a firearm. We ought to charge them both with armed robbery as soon as the loose ends can be tied up.' He glanced toward Detective Inspector Hedley. 'Which leaves you out in the cold as far as the abduction is concerned. They both deny having anything to do with it and we're short on evidence.'

'More than short, sir,' Hedley remarked gloomily.

'Have you interviewed Mrs Hammond again?'

'Yes. I'm afraid she wasn't exactly helpful. Said she'd told us everything she knew.'

'What about playing her recordings of Harrison's and Sidley's voices? She might recognise them.'

'I thought of that, sir, but she says she's hopeless at recognising voices unless there's something special about them and there was nothing distinctive about those of her kidnappers.'

'Does she still believe her husband was behind it?'

'Yes. And he equally strenuously denies it.'

Kershaw scratched his nose. There's definitely something fishy about that abduction. I shan't be happy until we've cleared it up.' Glancing at Cleave, he went on, 'I gather neither Harrison nor Sidley have said anything that lets Lumley off the hook?'

'Sidley simply says he's never heard of him . . . '

'That must be a lie for a start,' Kershaw broke in. 'Don't tell me he didn't follow Lumley's trial with considerable interest.'

'One would suppose so, sir,' Cleave agreed. 'As for Harrison, he admits there was someone else in the shop at the same time, but that's all. Says Fingle might have known more, but he doesn't.'

'Very convenient with Fingle dead. Also very unconvincing.'

Cleave nodded. 'Whoever roped Lumley in and for what purpose, Harrison's not saying.'

'It was a good day when we caught those two, but there's the hell of a lot more we need to know. Meanwhile, we'd better get down to some detailed co-ordination . . . '

Chapter 28

It was not long after Cleave had left the meeting and returned to his own office that he received a call from Rosa.

'I gather you have Harrison and Sidley under lock and key,' she said.

'They haven't yet been charged with robbery, if that's what you want to know,' Cleave replied with a slight note of irritation. He could guess why Rosa was calling him and he would have preferred not to talk to her.

'I take it they *will* be charged with the robbery?'

'Yes, when we've tied up a few loose ends.'

'May I ask if you've personally questioned them since they were detained?'

'You may and I have.'

'Have either of them said anything that helps Lumley?'

'Nothing.'

'Presumably they were asked about him?'

'Look, Miss Epton,' he said with a sigh, 'Would it really help you whatever they said?'

'How do you mean?'

'Lumley's inside for six years after a jury found him guilty of taking part in the robbery. Nothing Harrison or Sidley say can alter that.'

'I don't agree. If they supported his claim of innocence, it would be of considerable help to Lumley's cause.'

'You don't really believe that, do you, Miss Epton? The Home Secretary's never going to release him on their word. Criminals aren't exactly renowned for telling the truth.'

Rosa recognised the force of what Cleave was saying.

If prisoners were pardoned and released as easily as that, prison gates might as well be kept permanently on the latch. It was not uncommon for them to seek to exonerate one of their number and small effect it ever had on the authorities. Their motives for doing so were seldom beyond reproach.

Cleave went on, 'In my view, it doesn't matter very much what they say about Lumley. If they say he was in it with them, he stays where he is, and if they swear blind he wasn't one of the team, it'll be assumed they have an ulterior motive and nobody'll take any notice.'

'You obviously still believe that Lumley's guilty?'

'That's what the jury thought, Miss Epton.'

Rosa had known all along that it wouldn't be a simple matter proving Stephen Lumley's innocence, but her conversation with Inspector Cleave had starkly underlined the difficulties, particularly when he had gone on to tell her that Harrison was likely to use the dead Fingle as a shield behind which to take cover when he was pressed with too many awkward questions. He would adopt the line that Fingle had taken the answers with him to the grave.

It could be, she realised, that nothing would be resolved until Harrison and Sidley had themselves stood trial and that would be at least a year ahead. And even then there was no certainty that Lumley would be nearer a pardon.

That evening she sat with a large pad of paper on her knee and wrote down what she now regarded as the most plausible of all the theories she had formed. It meant going out on a limb in order to prove it and without any certainty of success. The time had come, however, to cast caution aside and to go for broke.

Her mind was made up. Let not the opposition think it had a monopoly in deviousness.

With this fortifying thought, she went to bed.

She found the address she was looking for without difficulty. It turned out to be a small modern block of purpose-built flats set in a pleasantly landscaped garden of shrubs and dwarf leafy trees, with an enormous ancient oak presiding in one corner.

183

There was a car park behind a screen of bushes. She locked her car and approached the front entrance. A woman ahead of her, laden with shopping bags, produced a key and unlocked the door, holding it open for Rosa.

Rosa thanked her and stepped inside the lobby which, she decided, had cheap pretensions to grandeur. She hadn't relished having to announce herself over the entryphone and now she had been spared that.

Flat Two was on the ground floor at the rear. A card in a slot beside the bell-push showed the occupant's name as Kestler. Rosa pressed the bell and waited.

She heard slight movement within and then the door was opened as far as its chain allowed and Carol Hammond's face appeared. She was frowning and wore a nervous expression.

'Aren't you Miss Epton?' she asked after a slight pause.

'Yes. May I come in and talk to you?'

'Are you alone?'

'Yes.'

Carol Hammond removed the chain and held the door open, closing and putting the chain back on as soon as Rosa was inside.

'This is my sister's flat. How did you know where to find me?' she asked, as she led the way into the lounge.

Rosa could hardly say that it had taken Ben a day's ferreting to discover the address.

'I read in one of the papers that you were staying with your sister in Croydon,' she replied, and was relieved when Carol didn't pursue the matter further.

She noticed an ashtray overflowing with cigarette ends, and that Carol lit a fresh cigarette as soon as she sat down. There was also a half-finished drink next to the ashtray. Carol picked up the glass and drained it.

Jumping up, she said, 'I'll just get myself another gin; then you can tell me why you've come.' Halfway across the room, she turned. 'By the way, do you want a drink?'

Rosa shook her head. 'No thanks.'

When Carol had sat down again, she cast Rosa a quizzical look and said, 'What can I do for you?'

'Do you really believe your husband had you abducted?'

'I'd never have believed it if I hadn't overheard my captors say so.'

'Why do you suppose he did so?'

Carol frowned. 'I've already made a full statement to the police and I can't really see what any of this has to do with you.'

'My interest is getting Lumley out of prison.'

'It was a great shock discovering that Stephen was involved in the robbery.'

'I take it you know that two other men have now been arrested?'

'Yes, the police came to see me. Heaven knows whether or not they've got the right men. Anyway, I made it clear there was nothing further I could do to help. There's no question of my being able to identify them, which was what the police were hoping. The men who came into the shop were both heavily disguised. It's ridiculous expecting people to have total recall of such incidents. Survival is all one is thinking of.'

'Do you think the robbery may have been a put-up job?'

Carol was in the act of lighting a fresh cigarette and gave Rosa a sharp look. 'I don't wish to be drawn into speculation. The police have all the facts and it's up to them what conclusions they draw.'

'But presumably you must wonder . . . '

'What I wonder is my concern.'

'Supposing the two men who've been arrested say that you instigated the whole thing, what would be your response?'

'It would be an outrageous lie, which would be laughed out of court.' She picked up her glass with a hand that noticeably trembled and took a deep gulp of gin and tonic.

'You know that Les Fingle was in touch with me shortly before his death?'

'Why should I know that?'

Ignoring the question, Rosa went on, 'He had a bad conscience about Lumley being charged with a crime of which he was innocent. That's why he made contact with my office. Unfortunately he provided someone with a motive to kill him. He had to be silenced before he could put others in jeopardy.'

'Why are you telling me this?' Carol broke in, reaching for her packet of cigarettes.

Rosa took a deep breath and went on, 'What you and others didn't know was that he had already told me the truth about the robbery.'

'How interesting for you!'

'You see, I now know that it was you who planned the whole thing and got Les Fingle to set it up. He got in touch with Harrison, who doubtless recruited Sidley.'

'And why should I arrange for my husband's shop to be robbed, Miss Clevertits?' Carol asked with a sneer.

'It's taken me longer than it should have to reach the answer to that,' Rosa replied equably. 'I always thought there was something fishy about the robbery, but the one thing I couldn't rationalise was that touch of realism with your husband being shot in the shoulder. Everyone kept on saying it happened in the general confusion and if one believed it was a put-up job, one had to assume the shot was meant to miss, but that your husband somehow strayed into the bullet's path. Then the truth dawned on me: the robbery was certainly a put-up job, but as a front. A front to murder. The bullet that struck him in the shoulder was intended to kill him. Your husband's murder was the object of the exercise. It would have freed you and left you a wealthy woman. Everyone, apart from your husband, would be happy, and he'd be in no position to express his feelings. Harrison and Sidley would get away with over £100,000 worth of jewellery and you'd still collect on the insurance. It was a well thought out plan; but badly executed.' The woman in front of her appeared visibly to shrink as she listened to Rosa's reconstruction with a mesmerised expression. 'As for your abduction,' Rosa went on, 'it's my guess that you arranged that yourself with the help of Harrison and Sidley. I imagine it was intended as a diversionary tactic to deflect suspicion that might be growing against yourself and direct

186

it firmly at your husband. The fact that you were abducted under the eyes of a lady who spent her time looking out of the window was obviously carefully planned. It struck me as odd at the time, as did your apparently fortuitous escape from the van that conveniently broke down in Epping Forest.'

Carol Hammond lay back in her chair with eyes closed. She looked totally exhausted. It was half a minute before she slowly opened them again.

'So what are you going to do about it?' she asked in a hoarse whisper, as she automatically reached for another cigarette.

'My only interest is in securing the release of an innocent client,' Rosa said. 'I need you to swear an affidavit that he wasn't part of the robbery.'

'But that means admitting . . . I could be sent to prison.' Her voice held a note of fear.

'I think you'd better accept that as inevitable,' Rosa observed dispassionately. 'It's a question of for how long.'

'What do you mean?'

'If you swear an affidavit on the lines I've stated, you need only admit to organising a robbery, which is a good deal less heinous than arranging your husband's murder. You must accept my word that I won't pass that on to the police.'

'Supposing I refuse to sign an affidavit?'

'I shall inform Inspector Cleave of everything that has passed at this meeting. The choice is yours, though I wouldn't have thought it was a very difficult one in the circumstances.'

'What reason can I give for plotting the robbery?'

'That's up to you. I suggest you get yourself a good lawyer.'

'Where do we do this affidavit?'

'We'll drive to my office now and you can swear it before my partner.'

Carol Hammond ground out her cigarette and gazed about the room with a distracted air.

'And will such an affidavit really bring about Stephen's release?'

Rosa let out a heartfelt sigh. 'I'm afraid not, but it'll be a beginning. It'll be the centre-piece of my petition to the Home Office.'

'Supposing he isn't released?'

'I'll go on fighting until he is. At least with your confession, justice will have been better served than once seemed likely.'

Carol Hammond flinched and covered her face with her hands. Then looking up she said in an urgent tone, 'I suppose you wouldn't defend me, would you?'

Rosa could hardly believe her ears and her mind grappled for a reply.

'No, I wouldn't,' she said eventually, in as restrained a voice as she could manage.

Epilogue

Carol Hammond's affidavit was the mere beginning of what turned out to be months of slogging endeavour with periods of total frustration. Despite Robin's warnings, Rosa had not foreseen how reluctant the establishment would be to admit a miscarriage of justice. It sometimes seemed that the officials concerned thought it preferable to keep an innocent person in prison than to undermine public confidence in the administration of justice.

The strain reduced Rosa to an almost permanent state of irritability. She would notice Stephanie ducking out of sight as she passed through the lobby and even Ben showed a tendency to keep his distance. At such times she would feel ashamed.

Lee Harrison, who in due course was found guilty of the murder of Leslie Fingle, had also agreed to swear an affidavit exonerating Lumley from any participation in the robbery. By then it had been decided not to prosecute him further in view of the life sentence he had received for the murder; but instead to call him as a witness against Sidley who still refused to admit anything. The police were at last satisfied that he had told them everything he knew about the robbery. They had been particularly interested to learn the name of the man who had been at the wheel of the getaway car. It was Alex Gage, a stock-car driver and long-time associate of Sidley's, who had been one of four people killed in a motorway pile-up a mere week after the robbery. Harrison, who said he had been against Gage's participation, clearly regarded his demise as justifying his opposition.

Eventually Sidley was convicted and given a ten-year sentence, which effectively brought their partnership in crime to an acrimonious end.

Carol Hammond pleaded guilty to conspiracy to commit robbery and was sentenced to five years for what the judge described as a wicked crime. He added that but for her plea and apparent remorse, she would have gone to prison for much longer. Her eloquent defending counsel painted a picture of a woman who had fallen from grace and lost everything she most valued in life.

Rosa had stayed away from court, but received a full report from Ben.

'To see her in the dock today,' he had said, 'you wouldn't have thought butter would melt in her mouth. I reckon she was dead lucky.'

So did Rosa in view of what she knew.

And still she fought on, paying dutiful visits to a despairing and, at times, painfully embittered Lumley.

It was the end of September before she was able to present a completed dossier to the Home Office. It then became apparent that that department wouldn't make any move until all the other defendants had been dealt with. Further frustration ensued. Meanwhile, Rosa had enlisted the support of Lumley's MP who proved to be an energetic ally.

Then one morning in December she received a letter saying that the Court of Appeal was, at the request of the Home Secretary, proposing to expedite Lumley's appeal, which had recently been lodged out of time with special permission.

This she took to be a promising sign, though, after so many setbacks, she kept her hopes in check.

In fact, the appeal court had clearly decided that the least said, the soonest mended. The presiding Lord Justice declared that since Lumley's trial many fresh matters had come to light, which could well have caused the jury to reach a different conclusion. In those circumstances his conviction could not safely be upheld and would be quashed, and he would be released forthwith.

Leaving the custody of the two prison officers sitting either side of him, he walked straight over to where Rosa was sitting and threw his arms around her.

The three judges observed the scene with judicial impassivity, while a flustered usher hurried to shoo them out of court.

It was raining when they came outside, but Ben, who had dashed ahead, had managed to find a taxi.

Back at the office where they were joined by Christine Lumley, Rosa opened a bottle of champagne. Robin was out, but she, Stephanie and Ben toasted their rather special client and his wife.

She was later to learn that Bernard Hammond had sent his nephew a substantial four-figure cheque. She felt that, in many ways, he had had a rough deal, though a payment of conscience money was not entirely amiss. He had, not surprisingly, instituted divorce proceedings, but was intending to carry on his business.

'Well done, my Rosa,' Robin said on hearing the news when he returned to the office.

'Have I been very difficult to live with these past few months?' she asked ruefully. 'Peter says he'd have stayed in Hong Kong if he'd known.'

'Anyone obsessed with a cause is apt to be a pain in the neck at times,' he said with a wry smile. 'At least yours was a just and worthwhile cause, so no complaints.' He paused a second. 'By the way, can you do a case for me tomorrow? I'm double booked.' Observing Rosa's expression, he quickly added, 'It's a plea of guilty to careless driving. A mere molehill of a case.'

'You mean that even I won't be able to make it into a mountain,' Rosa said with a laugh, as she re-filled their glasses with what was left of the champagne.